Wendy Rawlings

STORIES

Time for Bed

Louisiana State University Press
Baton Rouge

Published by Louisiana State University Press
Manufactured in the United States of America
LSU Press Paperback Original
First printing

DESIGNER: Mandy McDonald Scallan
TYPEFACE: Whitman
PRINTER AND BINDER: LSI

Library of Congress Cataloging-in-Publication Data

Names: Rawlings, Wendy, author.
Title: Time for bed : stories / Wendy Rawlings.
Description: Baton Rouge : Louisiana State University Press, [2019] | Series:
    Yellow shoe fiction
Identifiers: LCCN 2019008224 | ISBN 978-0-8071-7151-6 (pbk. : alk. paper) | ISBN
    978-0-8071-7225-4 (pdf) | ISBN 978-0-8071-7226-1 (epub)
Classification: LCC PS3618.A958 A6 2019 | DDC 813/.6—dc23

for Lucy and Sal

And they all lived

        happily

               ever

                     after.

CONTENTS

Time for Bed

Coffins for Kids!

The gunman didn't like redheads. Someone told Naomi afterwards. The gunman didn't like redheads, okay, but he liked, I don't know, what? Blasting the brains of seven-year-olds across a wall map of the United States made out of construction paper?

Spraying bullets at kids shoving coats inside lockers? Maybe he just didn't like maps of the United States. Maybe he had something against lockers. When he was a child had he cut the heads off rodents? That was a thing, wasn't it? An indicator of something gone wrong, early on? Naomi remembered her own childhood, stealing Mallomars from her mother's stash, learning to masturbate using Barbie's legs, shoplifting a lipstick from Macy's. Maybe she wasn't the numero uno best child in America, either. But growing up to blow away a bunch of third-graders with a semiautomatic weapon? Picking off redheads?

Oh, and he also didn't like girls. So Emily'd had two strikes against her. If only Naomi had birthed a brown-eyed boy, now she and Rick and the brown-eyed boy could leave New England forever, go live in New Mexico and grow edible cacti, reinvent themselves, get perma-tans. But no. Now Emily, with her wrong gender, wrong hair, was in the market for a coffin: *Hey Mom, could you get me a nice box to be buried in? All the other kids have one!* Rick had suggested cremation, but what parent puts her kid in an oven? Not a half-Jewish parent, that's for sure. So a nice box it would be.

She Googled *children's coffins*. Up came an image of a tattooed guy wearing a safety mask and doing something with a blowtorch. Asterisked beside the photo were the words *Free Consultation with Master Craftsman Brock Hunnicut. We Send Your Little Angel to Heaven "In Style."* Naomi lingered on the site, scrolling down to a photo of the guy with his wife. His dark beard reached nearly to his shirt pocket. Why had he put "In Style" in quotes? Maybe that was a trademarked phrase. The Custom Casket gallery showed coffins made to look like trains, like boats, like surfboards, like zebras. One had a Teenage Mutant Ninja Turtle's face on the lid, another had butterflies painted on it, another was camouflage with a deer's head on top and, attached to the side, a child-sized rifle. The sight of a firearm made Naomi gasp; she hadn't seen anything even resembling a gun since the Thursday Glen Belson decided he didn't like redheads.

The deer's-head coffin could ship in 24–36 hours.

She wondered if Brock Hunnicut took American Express.

When Naomi was thirteen, her favorite cousin had died of leukemia. Watching her father and her uncle weep openly at the funeral, Naomi swore she would never have kids. Instead she would have birds. Maybe a dog. She liked lizards. But when she was thirty-six, Rick convinced her to "take the goalie out," as he put it, and half a year later she was pregnant. That a child could die of leukemia had made Naomi an atheist. Who was crazy enough to believe in a God who was a total shithead? But Emily's death, and the deaths of her classmates Paul and Eleanor and Eleanor (all parents these days, it seemed, named their kids Eleanor), made Naomi reevaluate her atheism. A gunman wearing chain mail shooting up a third-grade class? That could only mean a God did exist, and he was a total jerk. And why hadn't anyone stopped a guy wearing freaking chain mail from entering a third-grade classroom?

"We thought he was doing a presentation on the Middle Ages," the principal told her and the other bereaved parents. Miss Oslansky wore polyester sheath dresses in primary colors with birds printed on them. Always birds. Once Rick had remarked that Miss Oslansky looked like she'd been extruded from a School-Principal-Making Machine. "We always do a unit on the Middle Ages," she said forlornly. "One is on the Black Death."

"A unit on the Black Death," Naomi repeated. She and the mothers of the Eleanors stared at each other's shoes. One of them looked as if she'd taken about nine different sedatives. The other bit at her fingernails so vehemently she drew blood. What did little kids need to learn about the Black Death for? Why couldn't they learn about something cheerful, like—well, like what? Science had its cheerful topics, ladybugs and the eradication of disease and whatnot, but history was a toughie. The Inquisition, the Holocaust, Hiroshima, the Nixon presidency. Slim pickings in the cheerfulness department. But if the curriculum was the Middle Ages, what about knights and nobles? Were knights and nobles cheerful? Knights wore chain mail, and chain mail brought her back to Glen the Gunman. Glen the Gunman had worn his chain mail as if for the battlefield, and his enemies were redheads and girls. His enemies were kids who still wet their beds (that ammonia smell wafting from her SpongeBob SquarePants sheets), and sucked their thumbs, and refused for months on end to eat anything but mashed potatoes and chocolate milk. Even if God was a total jerk, how could he set up such a one-sided matchup? Gunman versus Bed-Wetters! Heavily Armed Adult against Thumb-Suckers! Why couldn't jerk-face God direct Glen the Gunman to the middle of Kabul, where he could go head-to-blown-off-head with a suicide bomber?

Naomi thought about killing herself. *I kill me*, she whispered as she watered Emily's African violet. But first, she would order a coffin for Emily (the obvious choice would be SpongeBob SquarePants, though Emily had also been fond for a while of a TV show called *Pajanimals* that featured animals learning valuable lessons by traveling to whimsical lands. She had especially liked a character named Cowbella, a miniature pink cow who always seemed to be wearing the same pair of purple pajamas). But that had been when Emily was much littler. Hadn't it? Was it possible for a seven-year-old to have a period in her life when she was "much littler"? Naomi felt a burp of panic rise up in her. Soon she would forget what her daughter liked to eat, how her voice sounded, how her peed-on sheets smelled. That was why she had to kill herself. If she didn't go to heaven, she would just end up in a coffin underground right next to Emily, and the two of them could rot together. But if she in her atheist cynicism had been wrong all along, she and Emily would meet up at the Holy Gates or wherever were the crossroads of heaven, wear gossamer robes or whatever angels wore, eat manna tacos from some Nirvanian food truck, bed down on a cloud.

Naomi could braid Emily's red hair and make sure she learned about cheerful events in history, like *Brown v. Board of Education* and the Obama presidency. They could grow old together, or whatever you grew in heaven. Maybe you just grew wiser, and Emily could stay seven forever.

The coffin-maker had an 800 number. Good job: it wasn't something clever like 1–800–DEADKID. The grief counselor had told her she might struggle with a sense of unreality at times. At times? The grief counselor had told her to try to anticipate what might trigger feelings of grief. What wouldn't? "Grief produces a wide range of responses. Everyone expresses grief in his or her own fashion," the counselor said. "Really?" Naomi wanted to ask. Wouldn't uncontrollable weeping and suicidal ideation be pretty common ways? What were the others? Did some grievers go out and play a few rounds of golf? Drink a Mai Tai and watch the sun set? Go to Best Buy and price laptops?

"Would you be okay if I . . . weren't around?" she asked Rick over almond butter on rice cakes for dinner. Neither of them had the presence of mind to cook, and they were between casserole deliveries from friends.

"If you went on . . . vacation?" Rick asked. In the context of Emily's death the word seemed obscene, like eating dog meat in front of dogs.

"Sort of. More like a retreat." Naomi pictured her Hawaiian shirt turned into a noose. A nice New Mexico vista before she drove off the cliff.

"I could manage for a little while."

"Okay, cool." She tried to bring up the custom-coffin thing, but the words clogged her throat. Certain things you should never have to say.

A woman answered the phone. "How can we help?" she asked. Naomi remembered a photo on the website of a woman with her hair dyed partly pink. The "family liaison."

"I need a coffin," Naomi heard herself say. "For my kid." Immediately she felt she sounded too definite, too businesslike. I should be crying, she thought. I should be keening, rending garments.

"Honey, how soon do you need it?" the woman said gently.

"No giant rush," Naomi said. "We were part of that school massacre . . ." She trailed off, unsure what to say next.

"Which one?"

Which one? Had more than one lunatic mowed down bed-wetters and thumb-suckers this week? Naomi hadn't been watching the news; Rick had thrown a towel over the television, and she hadn't summoned the energy to remove it.

"Utah or New Hampshire? Or was it Vermont?"

"Utah?" Naomi asked.

Didn't they love kids in Utah? Didn't Utah have a law requiring you to have kids? "New Hampshire," she said.

"I'm deeply sorry for your loss. He was the one in chain mail, wasn't he? Not the Darth Vader."

"Not Darth Vader," Naomi said. "He was the other one." *Death is not the worst of evils.* That's what General John Stark wrote after *Live free or die* to his comrades celebrating the anniversary of the Battle of Bennington. He had a cold or something and couldn't go. Naomi had learned that in her seventh-grade unit on the American Revolution. But you know what? Death actually was the worst of evils. Not your own death—nope, that wasn't such a big song-and-dance. The worst of evils was your little girl's brains sprayed across the construction-paper poster of the United States by some nut wearing chain mail and carrying his own personal arsenal into Plymouth Elementary School. The worst of evils was Wayne LaPierre crawling out of whatever swamp he lived in to decry the tragedy of "gun-free zones," i.e., elementary schools.

The woman on the phone introduced herself as Jillian and said she would take down some information about the child's "final resting place." "How old was your little angel?" she asked.

Naomi felt a zap in her gut, like she'd swallowed a live wasp.

"Emily was seven." Seven years and three months and eleven days and four hours. "And what sort of theme are we thinking about?"

It could be anything, Naomi told herself. You can get a life-sized statue of Wayne LaPierre with his head shot off and his eyes poked out, roaches crawling out his eye sockets, each roach with a little speaker attached to its back that played the words *mea culpa* over and over again. Wait, his head couldn't be shot off, because that might be seen as condoning gun violence. Maybe a double-life-sized statue of Emily slicing his head off with a sword. That would be effective. All the news media in the entire world would cover the funeral. But Jesus, that would be exploiting the memory of her dead daughter. What the hell was wrong with her? What was she even thinking?

"I was thinking maybe Cowbella."

"We do Cowbella," Jillian said. "We can do her with her buddies or without. Do you want the whole crew? Squacky, the whole nine yards?"

"Definitely Squacky."

"Maybe they could be singing 'Sleeping Makes Me Feel All Right.' Though it's a little extra for the audio."

"I'll spring for it," Naomi said.

🐌

"I'm gonna go pick up the coffin," she told Rick. They were eating another casserole.

"You want me to come along?"

"I'll just whiz over and get it. Be back before you know." She didn't tell him it was in Texas, 2,038 miles away. She didn't tell him the coffin theme was *Pajanimals*. She didn't tell him she might on the way take a sunset detour off a cliff.

The next day, she loaded up a Styrofoam cooler with kombucha tea and a lot of cheese. Since the massacre, cheese had given her more comfort than she would have imagined cheese capable of. Those French were onto something. Maybe if the chain-mail guy and Wayne LaPierre got to eat more brie. . . . Of course, Wayne LaPierre hadn't himself committed a gun massacre, but in his activist zeal he seemed like kind of an advocate for gun massacres. All this enthusiasm over assault weapons was kind of unseemly, like a Christian showing up at Bergen-Belsen and saying what a great facility.

Plymouth, New Hampshire, was 549 miles from National Rifle Association headquarters. Naomi could do that distance in less than a workday. Not everyone knows that located beside the NRA HQ in Fairfax, Virginia, is a wheelchair-accessible shooting range open to the public. Fifteen shooting booths. More than nine million bullets had been fired at the facility. Did people in wheelchairs actually come to shoot AK-47s at paper targets? She could go talk to that square-headed LaPierre himself, shove Emily's blood-and-brain-spattered denim jumper in his face. Maybe she should get herself a gun to bring in—*Naomi, Get Your Gun!*—and scare the bejeezus out of everyone. Maybe she could dress in chain mail. Who knows, maybe they would welcome her if she showed herself to be one of them, a gun-totin' mama with attitude!

At a Cracker Barrel on I-95, Naomi wandered through the shop with its Mason jars full of gumballs, its Moon Pies and horehound drops in paper sacks (did anyone actually *buy* horehound drops in paper sacks?), its vintage bicycles and hacksaws hung from the ceiling. If Emily were here she'd want the lollipop shaped like a giant mustache. Naomi had refused, once, to buy it for her. How could she have forbidden her daughter the simple pleasure of a mustache lollipop? A wave of such rage and self-recrimination washed over her that she had to dig her fingernails into her palms to prevent an urge to crack a jar full of gumballs against her skull. Go eat eggs, she told herself.

She ate eggs. She played the triangular peg puzzle with the golf tees that sat next to the napkin dispenser. Emily had loved the peg puzzle. Why hadn't she bought Emily four hundred peg puzzles, four hundred mustache lollipops? And was that what grieving the death of a child in a consumer society came down to, hating yourself for all the crap you'd refused to buy your kid when she was alive and noodging you?

Fairfax was still four hours away. The FAQs page proved informative. Yes! Gift cards in any denomination could be purchased. No! No on-site instructors were available to provide firearm instruction, though the answer to this FAQ mentioned, helpfully, that a bulletin board with contact information for private instructors was available. Naomi could get lessons in firearm use right in the belly of the beast, inside the Holy Temple of the Right to Shoot Children at School itself! The facility was open seven days a week. Some FAQs she didn't even understand: *Does the NRA Range have someone to zero my rifle?* She was willing to bet that zeroing a gun didn't mean rendering it unable to shoot. Nope. It meant making sure the gun shot dead-center. You wouldn't want the aim to be off, though in the case of Glen the Gunman at Plymouth Elementary that didn't much matter, as he sprayed the room indiscriminately. A gunsmith could help you zero your rifle, but a gunsmith couldn't do anything about getting a hand or a handle on your gunman.

Gunmen, it turned out, run in any direction they want.

In the Cracker Barrel parking lot, she stretched her hips and drank kombucha, then turned on the radio and listened to a public station out of Philadelphia. The Quakers built their first meetinghouse in 1685. Those kooky Quakers with their beliefs that God resided in everyone and therefore you shouldn't commit violence because basically that was God you were socking in the nuts. Maybe being an atheist was too nihilistically lazy. Maybe she should become a Quaker. Could a Quaker learn to shoot at the NRA Range and then blow Wayne LaPierre's brains against the wall with the sign on it that reads NRA EXPLORE THE POSSIBILITIES? What were the possibilities to which that sign referred? Did Emily's untimely death at ten in the morning, right after she finished playing "Do You Hear What I Hear?" and put away her recorder, count as a possibility to explore?

As she neared Fairfax, she began to think maybe she should pick up the coffin first, then go to the shooting range. Maybe she could lug the coffin in there to show them her custom Cowbella. How heavy could a seven-year-old's casket be? She felt herself chickening, a word she and Emily and Rick had invented to refer to that shrinking feeling when you were about to bail on a plan. No, bringing the coffin would be too histrionic; it would get her thrown out. Better to go undercover. She would be the puffy-eyed warrior, the de-motherified mother of none learning to wield a gun.

The range was weirdly hidden under the parking deck, like a survivalist's bunker. Naomi paused in front of a large emblem of an eagle squatting on crossed rifles atop a badge printed with a United States flag. Could eagles actually squat? Maybe it was preparing to take flight, the crossed rifles gripped in its yellow talons. Maybe it was headed off to the suburbs to deliver some more firearms to psychotic personality types, angry white trigger-happy boys with Confederate flag collections.

The door opened onto a pristine lobby with a curved counter and glass display cases full of boxes of bullets bright as Good & Plentys and Mike and Ikes. A sylphlike blonde in something like a hacking jacket greeted her.

"I was hoping to see the range," she said.

"Are you looking to shoot?" the Sylph asked.

"Eventually. I was thinking I'd start by looking and then finish up with shooting. Shooting would be the finale," she said stupidly. "If I could borrow a gun."

"We don't lend. You didn't bring yours?"

"Mine's in the shop." Naomi offered what she hoped was a beseeching look. "You sell them? I could buy one, like, just a little one to tide me over." Till it comes back from the shop, good as new like a Subaru tune-up.

"You have to bring your own," the Sylph said. "Those are the rules."

So the NRA had rules. It wasn't the Wild West out here in Fairfax; you couldn't just show up and expect them to equip you with a firearm. Gunland had its own laws, no exceptions, not even if your kid had been blasted to eternity by a heavily armed kook!

"I just kind of wanted to see the place," she said. "It's been a dream of mine. I drove here from New Hampshire."

"Well, you should've said! It's quiet today—I'll give you a tour." The Sylph stepped from behind the counter. She wore black pumps with extraordinarily high heels, so that she towered over Naomi in sneakers.

The Sylph's name was Tina. The Sylph liked to shoot. The Sylph had been working for the NRA for nine years.

"Did you ever shoot anyone?" Naomi asked.

"I only shoot to kill," Tina said, which Naomi took to mean no.

They walked into a fluorescent-lit room with numbered booths separated by Plexiglass walls the size of doors, each one like a bathroom stall open at the back. Only one booth was occupied, by a man Naomi could only think of as furry. He wore safety glasses and blue earphones, and his bearded face looked more bearlike than human. With an enormous rifle he was blasting the crap out of a blue drawing of a person on a paper target. When they stepped into his peripheral vision, he stopped and took off his earphones. "Ladies," he said.

"What'd that guy ever do to you?" Tina asked. Both she and Furry laughed.

"That's Obummer," Furry said, and the two of them laughed again.

"I voted for Obama," Naomi said. "Twice."

"Sorry," Furry said, and Naomi knew he meant he was sorry she voted for Obama twice, not sorry for insulting her. This had all been a mistake. Her motives hadn't been clear. What had she thought she'd do, choose some random gun supporters and unload her grief on them? Use Emily to try to guilt-trip them into locking up all the guns and throwing away the key?

"My daughter was killed by a school shooter," she blurted. It was the only bullet she had.

The three of them stood looking at the pockmarked paper target.

"Well, that's a hellacious situation, and I'm very sorry to hear it." Furry put out his hand and grasped Naomi's arm for a moment. *That is an arm that just shot a gun,* Naomi thought.

"We all need to protect ourselves," Tina said, in a voice Naomi recognized as NRA spokesperson voice, commercial voice-over voice, don't-you-dare-argue-with-me voice.

Protect ourselves? Naomi thought. She felt herself riding over the lip of sanity and into something uncontained: an ocean of toxic junk, a vat of dismembered body parts, a galaxy of creosote and ash. What had she neglected to do in the protection department? Get a pint-sized bulletproof vest for her kid? Tuck a hand grenade in her lunchbox? Hire bodyguards to follow her from art to gym? Why hadn't she thought of any of these things before Emily had her brains blown out? How could a mother be so negligent? Here she had been coaching her daughter on the intricacies of Common Core Math, when she should have been teaching her how to dodge a bullet. Or a hail of bullets.

How did one dodge a hail of bullets?

For a long moment, Naomi pictured herself collapsing on the highly polished floor, making her messy grief the NRA's problem. Furry and the Sylph would kneel awkwardly beside her, and she'd let her tears and snot dribble onto their capable arms, those arms that were so good at aiming and shooting, loading and reloading. The Sylph would get her a Sprite while Furry stroked the side of her head. They weren't bad people, these gun-lovers, these rifle associators, these keepers and bearers of arms. They had just confused the importance of one kind of arms for another. From Naomi they would come to understand the nature of their confusion, would come to see how much more important than firearms human arms were—human arms with tattoos of anchors and nudes on them, and wiry black hairs, and warts, and blemishes, and carcinomas from too much tanning, and scars from cutting and suicide attempts. Once Naomi made them understand, all those arms wouldn't want to aim guns at anyone.

Those arms would lay down their arms and learn to knit. Or juggle.

Furry laid a hand on Naomi's forearm. "What I would suggest for you," he said, "is the Glock 26. People call it the Baby Glock. It's subcompact."

The Sylph nodded. "It's not the most attractive, but you can't beat it for reliability."

Naomi gave her companions a close look. They wore twin expressions of concern. Even though a gun had killed her kid, and guns would continue to kill kids, these folks weren't joking; Furry and Sylph wanted to give her good gun-buying advice. In the universe they inhabited it was hellacious that her kid had been blown away, but they, like good Americans, were looking toward the future, when she might not be anyone's mother ever again, but could protect herself with a Baby Glock—not attractive, not warm or affectionate, but reliable. *A reliable baby.* What more could you ask for?

Portrait of My Mother's Head on a Plate

It was the denouement of our family. Our nuclear ever-after, my sister said. I was in college, my first year. Small, liberal arts, Connecticut, quadrangle. From that year's *Guide to Colleges* (you always end up reading these later): "All 1,700 students combined are one type of student. According to one alumnus administrator: 'upper-middle-class, conventional, and athletic.'" *I* was upper-middle-class, conventional, and athletic. Ditto my sister. We were prepared for the bourgeois scripted *telos* of our parents' lives: wooden-boat acquiring and restoring (our father); shopaholism, overreliance on antidepressants (our mother).

Then our mother left our father for a woman.

We were disappointed. Disappointment, I said, was the predominant emotion we were feeling. Who did I say this to? It must have been myself, as at college I spoke of this to no one.

On the phone, that autumn, my sister and I made lists.

"10 Reasons Why Our Mother Should Keep Being Our Mother"

1. Because she's our mother.
2. Because she's our mother. . . .

She moved out. She moved out of our house on an isthmus on Long Island with the screened-in porch facing the water. She moved out with the stained glass windows she'd helped us cut and solder, and the rugs she'd helped us hook, and the planters she'd helped us macramé. She, our high-school art teacher and the high-school art teacher of all our friends and enemies, moved out. She took a sofa and a lamp and a teapot (THE teapot) and the matching suitcases and the dresser with her makeup in the top drawer and the spare change I, when I was younger, filched. She took the mandala on the wall in the living room and framed photos of Emily at Kutscher's Camp Anawana and of me at my senior prom with the junior I'd had to ask who'd showed up wearing a red tuxedo jacket that made him look like the maître d'. She took the irregular pieces of pottery our father had never liked anyway because you couldn't put them in the microwave.

She scrammed.

She up-and-wented it.

She left, my father said, and built her little Rome someplace else. He FTD'd lavish bouquets to my mother's little Rome.

He got little notes back: "Thank you for the beautiful flowers." "Thank you again for the once again beautiful flowers."

I called my sister almost every day from my dorm. We polled each other: If you were our mother, would you rather be in a loving relationship with

a) Our father, who FTDs lavish flowers

b) The cafeteria lady in a hairnet

"But those aren't the terms of it," our mother said. "You said 'loving relationship,' but what if only one of those two entities offered you a loving relationship? Lavish flowers are after all only a momentary substitute for or maybe the word I'm looking for is *symbol of* a loving relationship."

"She only wears the hairnet at work," our mother said.

✑

Our mother took us to lunch. We went to the Greek place, our family's favorite lunch and dinner spot where the owner always puts his lit cigarette on the edge of the table and kisses Emily, me, our mother.

Now we thought, "There's a *man* kissing our mother."

We wanted to see if she would flinch. That's where our heads went, without us trying.

Our mother ordered us glasses of wine.

"It's the middle of the day," Emily said.

"Then don't drink yours," our mother said.

"Look," our mother said to us next, across our three wines, "I'm still your mother. Same me. Same smile"—she smiled—"same ten pounds overweight, same hair."

"You colored your hair," Emily said.

"Same hair," our mother said. "Just lighter and shorter."

"I would like saganaki and a side order of hummus and the whole-wheat flat pitas, fried, and extra yogurt sauce and onions on the side," I told the waitress.

It was what our father always ordered.

"I miss our family, too," our mother said, when the waitress went.

"We want it back," we said. We missed our straight mother and the other hair and our father who drank one gin-and-tonic each night instead of four.

✑

Jarvis Hall, Room 103. Phil Collins's "In the Air Tonight" on the radio. Wayne Gretsky hockeysmiling it down from the poster on the wall. Keith Sleator hockeysmiling it on his bed in the dim four-thirtyish late-autumn light. It's before dinner. It's before Mondale-Ferraro lose the election. Beside Keith I'm sitting in a T-shirt that says *Geraldine Ferraro: It's About Time!*

I'm still so interested in how this is the person with whom I've lost my virginity.

In his own T-shirt (forgettable slogan: maybe "Choate Hockey") and vertical-striped boxer shorts (I'm sitting here having an ordinary conversation with a man wearing only boxer shorts!), he's fascinating to me, though he's not doing anything other than occasionally humming along with the radio and trying on his hockey mask. He is, as my mother would say, filling the whole frame. I'm interested in the way different parts of his body smell. When I give him a hand job (he has taught me this) and he urges my head down toward the opening in his boxers, I'm more interested than afraid. "A lot of guys think you don't like them or you're grossed out by them if you don't let them come in your mouth," he tells me. I'm getting an education here. Gamely I entertain the possibility of letting him come in my mouth sometime. "Okay, *Geraldine*," he says, and kisses me. It's true, I point out that if Mondale-Ferraro win we might have a female president one day because presidents do after all sometimes get assassinated. "I'm quaking in my boots at the thought," he says and holds the back of my head when he kisses me again and slides his hand slowly down my ponytail, which I like and wish he would do more, though I don't ask for fear I'll make him self-conscious about it because it's a gesture that's tender. Unbidden as he's kissing me I get a picture in my head of my mother kissing the mouth of the cafeteria lady and of my mother reaching up tenderly to remove the cafeteria lady's hairnet. "A ponytail is a good way to wear long hair," Keith says, "and I don't mean to be crude but it's a good way to wear your hair if you're going to give a blow job."

⚘

Oh, indeed, I say to Emily, it would be an unwelcome thing if anyone at this college, even the nicest diplomat's daughter, future governor of Massachusetts, debutante who has appeared in *W* magazine, or what have you, found out that our mother left our father for the cafeteria lady at the public high school we attended.

"Attend," Emily says. "Am attending."

"But by now don't you think, realistically, that every ear-possessing person at Paul D. Schreiber High School already knows about our mother and the cafeteria lady?" I ask.

"No," Emily says, lying for both of us.

Poor old Emily—poor old, I say, for the following reason: she's trying to get into her choice of small liberal arts college, but she keeps edging toward and away from the idea of writing her admissions essay.

She takes a poll. It's still the era of polling, for Emily and me.

If you were me, she says, would you

a) Take advantage of your mother leaving your father for a woman by writing a troubled but ultimately redemptive (if falsely so) essay about what you learned from your mother leaving your father for a woman after twenty years of marriage?

b) Not be such a hypocrite and write instead on how being a volunteer in the pediatric oncology unit at Long Island Jewish changed your life or how working summers on a fishing boat with your father and shucking oysters that gave you permanent calluses changed your life?

"Which one?" she says.

"Which one do you think you want to write? I mean intuitively."

"I don't think I can write the kind of essay about Mom that they would want to read."

It should not, you are saying, matter. You who venerate love, you whose best friends (some of them) are gay, you who read college admissions essays. It could be the Prince of Wales that our mother fell in love with. It could be the assistant principal of our high school, the one with glaucoma who wears dark glasses all the time. It could be the New York Yankees, the ghost of Edgar Allan Poe, the scales of Justice, the left foot of Daniel Day-Lewis in *My Left Foot*. A ferret, a viper, a litter of gerbils. Botticelli's *Venus* (the painting, not the person) or Botticelli's dogs who disembowel his pursued woman. The icing on cakes, the white rind on brie, the head on stout. The smile of despair on the face of

Emma Bovary when she finds the engraved cigarette case belonging to a gentleman after the ball at La Vaubyessard and realizes how truly much she hates her husband (I was taking a nineteenth-century novel course). The walnut-sized tumor—benign!—the doctor removed from one of our mother's breasts.

Did it matter who or what our mother loved? We took a poll.

It mattered only at night when we were trying to go to sleep and the moving pictures played in front of our closed or opened eyes: our mother with the cafeteria lady. It mattered in line at the IGA when the cashier made a face at Emily, and Emily took the half gallon of ice cream home and ate it until her teeth hurt from cold and then threw up in the toilet.

It mattered in the dining hall when my roommate told our table she was going to the Gold and Silver in New York and I said, "What's the Gold and Silver?"

"You know, a coming-out ball."

"Huh," I said.

It mattered at breakfast, lunch, and dinner, shower time and sleep time, the times when I had sex (I don't know if Emily, yet, was having sex) or masturbated (tried). Also it mattered whenever we thought about our mother, our father, our past, our present, our hometown, our relatives, our friends, our future, marriage, men, death, the beach, or literature.

Other than that it didn't matter.

ॐ

"What is it with you and Geraldine Ferraro?"

In Keith's room, me typing Keith's paper for History 101. This is before personal computers. I'm typing it on onionskin paper slid into a Smith-Corona electric typewriter.

"It's history. We never had a female vice president."

"Like duh, I don't know that."

"It's just something I think would be great."

"It's just"—him up on an elbow on his bed, watching me at his desk—"You make too big a deal out of it."

I understand: This is the thing I've done wrong at college, in any number of ways.

The temperamental correcting cartridge I have to slide in and out of the typewriter every time I make a mistake. The physical whap-whapping sound of the keys hitting ink onto the paper.

I say a naïve thing next: "We're in college. We're supposed to be interested in things."

"Okay, Geraldine."

After that, whenever we see each other, crossing the quad: "Hey, Jerr-ul-deen."

Second semester I sign up for Intro to Drawing. We draw wine bottles

> bowls
> fruit
> fruit in bowls
> fruit and scissors and bottles on a piece of cardboard
> a ladder
> other kinds of bottles

I name all my drawings.

> "Still Life with My Mother's Soft White Arms and 3
>   Pieces of Fruit"
> "Portrait of My Mother's Head on a Plate"
> "Disemboweling of the Pursued Woman"
> "Still Life"
> "Still . . . Life"

I mail them to Emily, who says, "I don't see why it's a portrait of her head on a plate."

"You're being too literal." This is a criticism our mother has on occasion leveled when teaching us about art.

"The ellipses are pretentious and self-pitying," Emily says.

"You ripped off Botticelli with the pursued/disemboweling thing," she says. "What it looks like is two bottles and a ladder," she says.

❧

Saturday night, early spring, Alpha Delta Phi house. Sand trucked in for the floors. Limbo pole. Flaming torches that are probably violating a fire code. Grain-alcohol punch in garbage cans with dry ice billowing out of them.

Keith, hand grazing my arm: "There's probably a little piece of you that still wants to fuck me."

Me, in a flowered wrap skirt, sunglasses on my head—I've overdone it again: "You're probably right about that."

Keith: "You probably could if you wanted to."

Me: "I probably could."

There's a guy in tropical-patterned shorts waiting off in my peripheral vision somewhere, a Styrofoam cup of punch in each hand. I'm counting on the music being too loud for him to hear.

Keith: "You don't wear your Geraldine propaganda anymore."

Me: "That's because the Democrats lost the election, you asshole."

Keith: Says nothing, but puts his hand under my hair and leaves it for a moment on my neck.

Even as I'm pleased about calling him an asshole, I know what's going to happen later, back at the dorm.

❧

Emily calls to tell me where she got her acceptances. All on the same day, a torrent of thick envelopes.

"That's impossible," I say.

"Okay, I got them over a few days. I've been saving it up to call you."

She gets accepted to all the trust-fund-kid schools, all the schools with the nice and fancy names that you are proud to wear on a sweatshirt. Better schools, even, than the one I attend.

"So which one's it going to be?" I ask.

Long, worrisome silence from her end.

"I wish I'd applied to places in California. In California no one would find out about Mom."

If you're not familiar with the story, Botticelli's *Disemboweling of the Pursued Woman* doesn't completely make sense, though anyone can have a visceral reaction to the naked woman being attacked by dogs in the center of the canvas. Our mother told us this the first time she showed us the painting. We liked *The Birth of Venus* better, but we had to listen to our mother's spiel. "When they're finished disemboweling her, the woman gets up and the dogs chase and disembowel her all over again. It's the knight's"—she pointed to the knight, not looking very happy about the proceedings—"punishment for committing suicide for love."

Our mother does not believe you should throw yourself to the dogs for love. "You love someone for as long as you can in the best way you can, and if you come to the end of that you should move on and love whatever's next." She says this when I call her from college.

I can hear how my voice on the phone is gravelly and uncommitted to anything.

I'm putting on my flat affect, which I use these days for a) our mother and b) Keith.

"What is this person's name again you've been involved with?
"Keith."
"And what is it he said to you?"
"He didn't say anything specific. He's just giving me the run-around."
"Meaning what?"
"Meaning he'll sleep with me but not talk to me, like, in daylight."
"Well, that sounds like a real stick between the eyes," our mother says.

࿐

Jarvis Hall, Room 103, end of spring term.

"My mother says you're taking advantage of me."

I don't know why I say this to Keith, as it's not even a semi-accurate paraphrase of "Well, that sounds like a real stick between the eyes." I'm not even sure what our mother is getting at, precisely, with the phrase "stick between the eyes." Maybe a thing that hurts in some way that's unnecessary.

Keith is hanging up his button-down shirts that he just got back from the cleaners.

"What did you tell your mother about you and me?"

"That you'll sleep with me but won't talk to me in daylight."

"Right now, I'll inform you, it happens to be daylight, and last I checked we were talking."

"You're being overly literal."

He interrupts the putting away of the shirts and comes over and puts his arms around me. At previous times I would prefer not to recall he has made disparaging remarks about imperfections of my body and face, imperfections that aren't passing or correctible such as blemishes or flabbiness but more permanent, such as the fact that my face is asymmetrical and my breasts small. There are some funky things about his face and body (notably, a wandering eye that is a real wandering eye, not a metaphor, and makes him look a little crazy or at least medicated at certain instants), but I say I would never mention them to him.

"Maybe you should," he says.

"To what end?"

"To the end of us just being honest with each other, as we are fuck-buddies."

I tell him that's a disgusting word and I would prefer almost any other, even "casual friends who sleep together."

"That's unwieldy," he says.

He leads me over to the bed, and we take off our shirts. His floor looks almost artfully layered with clothing that has been worn and discarded—you could get from one side to the other without your feet touching bare floor. I've been known to do Keith's laundry, and I mention laundry now as we sit and lift our feet to slide our jeans off.

Keith drags his fingers along the part of my ribcage that protrudes. I'm holding in my stomach to emphasize the effect.

"What are you talking about laundry for?"

"I saw the clothes on the floor. It just reminded me."

He pushes at my stomach and tickles me. He knows I'm ticklish, will laugh until I'm gasping for air. He makes me laugh until I'm gasping. Then he has me lie on my back. On his hands and knees, he travels over my body, kissing and touching me.

"Still thinking about laundry?"

"No."

"What are you thinking about?"

He's looking straight down at me with his one good eye and his one eye that's indifferent. There's the heat of two faces close together. Mouths that might just as easily kiss or spit.

"Geraldine?"

"I don't think about her!"

A warm burst of Keith's breath in my face. He's laughing. "I don't think about her, either."

He proceeds to do the things I'm by now used to him doing when we're in bed. I try to come up with something that would be the right thing to be thinking about while he's doing this. But I don't think so much during these episodes. I hold myself in place. The piece of paper slid into the typewriter on the desk doesn't think.

We make love, not inventively and not in a way that I would say is especially loving, though I would be lying or at the very least willfully overlooking something if I didn't admit of some gratification on both our parts. I forget for a while about time passing and about my mother, two things I like forgetting about.

I'll go on like this for a number of years, passive and compliant in bed as a patient on a gurney. I'll go to bed with a lot of men who imagine they have a passion for technique. Thoughts will come to me as I lie on their flannel sheets, the primary colors and Tartan plaids men favor, the sleeping bags unzipped to improvise comforters. Maybe this is what our mother's life was like with our father, I'll think as the square of afternoon light in the window goes dark on a Saturday and the man beside me drops off to sleep. Maybe I'll end up like our mother. But in all the ways I fear or hope to end up like her, I won't.

Tics

This arrangement is new and could go badly. My mother, her partner Amy, my father, his fiancée Dawn, my older sister Jane, my younger sister Phyllis, and Dawn's three sons, Glen, Garrett, and Greg, seem to like each other well enough, if in a strangers-making-polite-conversation way. Dawn is the kind of person who gives her sons names with the same first initial. Our mother is the opposite of that kind of person. At dinner when our families meet, Jane announces she has joined the Church of Scientology.

"I don't know what to say about this," my mother says.

Phyllis says this is probably a good time to announce she has joined the Church of Jesus Christ of Latter-Day Saints. "Don't say it's a mouthful," she warns.

"And you?" my mother asks.

I nod no. Of late all I've joined is Weight Watchers, and no one needs to know that.

There's an air of forced Christmas gaiety at this blended-family function, maybe because like in *The Brady Bunch* there are three daughters and three sons, maybe because the straight parent and stepparent are trying hard to seem not merely tolerant but supportive of the gay parent and stepparent. Everyone has already stepped on everyone else's toes; now it's time to enjoy the cold shrimp and glasses of tawny port my father and I like and the white zinfandel that by some coincidence both Amy and Dawn drink.

"I'm worried," my mother says to me in a fake *sotto voce*. "Those are cults. They'll take all your money and change your values."

"I was ready to have my values changed," Phyllis says. Phyllis with her Jewish name my mother insisted on, her big breasts like my mother's that she's ashamed of, her dyslexia that made school so difficult.

My father says we're adults now and capable of making our own decisions. He's taking apart a blender I broke a while back and making his remarks in a halting monotone, like someone doing a bad job reading from a teleprompter.

"I wish you wouldn't take that apart on the dining room table," my mother says.

This is my mother's house now, my mother's table.

⟋₰

Glen is seventeen. He says he'd like some tawny port, and my dad pours him a glass. He swirls it in the snifter with great seriousness. There's something a little bit wrong with Glen. At regular intervals he twitches, and there's an accompanying click in his throat he doesn't seem able to control. It's astonishing to me that my sisters and I don't know basic things about our stepparents and stepbrothers. There has been little communication between us and our parents. I would ask my father, but I'm three-quarters sure he hasn't noticed anything unusual about Glen, which would probably depress me more than finding out Glen has a rare neurological disease. Glen appears smart for a seventeen-year-old, and also savvy in a way that my father and I are not and have never been and never will be.

At some point, I'm sent to the convenience store for beer, and Glen says he'll come with me. He kicks jauntily out to my car in light rain. "Raining on my suede boots," he says several times, half-singing. "My suede booties. I ordered them direct from London."

I let him drive my Honda. He sings under his breath, some old blues song. Back when my mother was a schoolteacher, she would have described Glen as the kind of kid who was able to amuse himself. I look carefully at him. He has a heart-shaped face with thin, very red lips that look painted, a doll's lips. When we're talking and he turns toward me to smile (he does this a lot), I see his two front teeth are discolored, as if someone has written on the ivory surface with white chalk. I decide he has a calcium deficiency.

"We should get something funny, like malt liquor." He chuckles. "Dawn drinking malt liquor," he says. Then he sings, "Dawn drinking that malt liquor in the morning." He makes the hitching sound in his throat and his head twitches.

"I have to ask you what's wrong with you." I realize what I've meant to say has come out wrong.

Glen hums and bumps his wrists against the steering wheel. "Don't worry about it. I have Tourette's. I tic all the time."

"It must drive you crazy." I'm wondering if he ever yells curse words, the way people with Tourette's do in the movies.

"I think it drives everyone crazy but me. I don't notice it."

I find this impossible to believe and decide he must be trying to downplay or show off. It occurs to me that my new stepbrother might want to impress me.

We buy beer and a forty-ounce bottle of Colt 45. As I'm paying I know Glen and I are going to go somewhere and drink it. The town where I grew up, the town in which I'm now buying my first-ever bottle of malt liquor, is on the north shore of Long Island, an isthmus in the Sound. A dusting of new snow has blown across the water and settled on the rocky shore of Ransom Beach. For the first time, as Glen's pulling into the parking lot, I notice that Ransom is a sinister name for a beach. A girl from my high school was killed by her boyfriend and stuffed into the trunk of a car in this lot.

Glen's telling me that he wears the same clothes every day. We've opened the Colt 45.

"That's disgusting. How often do you wash them?"

"No, dummy: I have five white oxford-cloth shirts, five pairs of black dress slacks, two dark blazers, and I rotate them. The boots are too expensive at this point for me to own more than one pair."

I'm drinking malt liquor with a dandy. The dandy's use of the word "dummy" pulls me back from some unfamiliar precipice; I'm reminded he's my seventeen-year-old stepbrother.

Glen claims e. e. cummings wrote a novel. He knows this because e. e. cummings is his favorite poet, other than Baudelaire. I decide I'll call Glen "e. e." from now on. Or maybe just "eeee," I say.

"Why don't you just call me cummings?" He licks his lips. There's a double entendre in this for both of us. I feel my vagina get hot. There is no denying it.

"The enormous room," Glen says. His face has gotten close to mine, and for a moment I don't understand that he's telling me the title of the e. e. cummings novel. I picture the two of us on an enormous mattress, no matter the size of the room. He puts his hand on my shoulder and kisses me in a tender, exploratory way. In a moment I've let his tongue wander into my mouth. Then I ruin it by pulling back and gasping that I'm twenty-seven and furthermore his stepsister.

He takes my hand and holds it between both of his. "Okay, I see the age thing, though it doesn't bother me. The step thing, though, it's a social construct. We met each other because our parents are getting married. That's the extent of it."

On the way home, he keeps his hand over mine on my left leg. "I'm so glad we talked," he says. I realize he is acting like the older person, whereas I'm the mute inexperienced child. I still feel hot between my legs, which are now trembling. Before we get out of the car, he turns and looks me in the eye. "If I had a condom, I would've made love to you."

Back in my mother's house he acts perfectly normal, except for what I perceive as a certain courtliness toward my sisters and me. The malt liquor combined with the incident in the car have made me woozy, so I beg off and lie down in my childhood room, which is still decorated with a Jim Dine poster depicting hearts that seem to dissolve into confetti.

Of course he will come to my apartment in Queens, because he's seventeen and in high school and his bedroom's next door to my father and Dawn's. We'll talk about how my father likes to start making chicken curry with golden raisins early on Sunday morning, so that the smell you wake up to is Indian. How my father's other favorite meals to make are a head of cauliflower swimming in melted cheese or a head of broccoli swimming in same (these are recipes he learned during food rationing in World War II, when his family in London had no meat). How my father keeps a portable fish smoker on the back steps and is constantly trying to foist smoked whitefish off on his kids. First I was his kid; now his kid is Glen.

"He's a nice guy. My father used to hit us."

"He *is* a nice guy," I agree, though something in me wonders if I'm sitting with Glen on my bed in nothing but a shirt and crimson panties because on some level I'm angry with my father. Glen's wearing the same white oxford-cloth shirt he always wears, this time with black jeans and black loafers. I've unbuttoned the shirt halfway and can see his hairless chest and one pale brown nipple. It occurs to me I could vomit or faint.

From his pants pocket he pulls a plastic strip of condoms long enough to be a sight gag. I let out a sick-hearted little laugh.

"Just to be on the safe side," Glen says.

We make love in every way possible, by which I mean we try out a variety of positions, but also a variety of emotional stances. We make love. We have sex. We fuck.

We get brutal and then we stop the brutality and caress each other's bodies with our fingertips. I lie on my stomach and show him how to put his hand inside me and make me come, which delights him. The pedagogical aspect of all this arouses us further; I have never before been the expert in bed with a man. Afterwards, Glen goes out to the crummy Stop & Shop in my neighborhood and comes home with ingredients for chicken cordon bleu, green salad, candied pecans, and roasted red potatoes. "You'll have to go out for the wine," he says. As he cooks, he sings, "Woke up this morning with my head in my hand, come on children, come on children." From across the room I catch his eye, and he gives me a little nod that might be a tic.

After we eat, we make love in the shower, where he soaps my shoulders and breasts and between my legs. "You have a nice body," he says, as if this is a fact he's simply reporting. No man has ever told me I have a nice body. The sex has turned me inside out, sex with a seventeen-year-old more tender and honest than sex with men my own age or even men much older. The man I dated most recently, a classical composer, was too caught up in his work to pay much attention to me. I realize Glen can give me his attention because his only responsibility is high school, which he hates.

He takes the train in and stays overnight, telling his mother and my father that he's staying with a friend he met "jamming." My father was laissez-faire with us growing up, so I'm not surprised. From all the sex I develop a urinary tract infection so painful that I send Glen to buy me Uristat from the Stop & Shop. It numbs the pain some, but turns my urine a rusty color that makes me feel old and used. "Come and see," I say, and Glen pads obediently into the bathroom. "Cool," he says. He's open to seeing the aesthetic merit in everything. While I wait for anti-biotics to heal my infection, he reads to me from his copy of *The Enormous Room* and plays blues riffs on a keyboard he brought from home. We smoke his pot. We write captions for *The New Yorker* cartoon contest. We watch *The Aristocrats*, which consists of comedians each telling their version of the same joke. Glen laughs at all of them. If you were to meet Glen, you'd understand instantly why a movie consisting entirely of comedians telling their versions of the same joke epitomizes his life philosophy. This is a person who never tires of his London suede boots. "I'd like very much to be a comedian, if I were funny. It's regrettable to me that I'm not funny," he says as he cues up *The Aristocrats* again. He seems to have an extraordinarily well-developed sense of his talents and shortcomings, better than most adults I know. I wonder if the Tourette's has given him a clearer eye to his limitations. With a twitch like that, he could never be a brain surgeon.

I'm speaking about this love affair as if it takes place over weeks or even months. So far what I've told occurs between Boxing Day and three days after New Year's, when I'll go back to work and Glen to school. I work in Midtown at a trade-magazine publisher. I write copy for *Sporting Goods Business*, but I'm hoping to be moved over to *Premium Incentive Business*.

"I can't even imagine what they do over at *Premium Incentive*." Glen's sitting on my bed with his knees pulled up to his chest. He's wearing boxer briefs and his unbuttoned white oxford.

I lie next to him and let one leg splay out, hoping my pose is suggestive. I still haven't completely grasped the fact that, to a seventeen-year-old boy, any pose is suggestive, especially as I'm currently and often naked. I run my hand over my pubic hair and notice how happy I am, how free of want. Glen wriggles out of his boxer briefs and takes his cock in his hand and guides it into me with one gesture.

There's often no need for foreplay between us; all the time we're together is foreplay, when Glen's singing the blues and cooking flank steak for our dinner.

"Let's just go on and on like this," he says.

As if he's challenging me to say out loud the reasons why we can't.

᭞

It's boring to be back at work, but I'm grateful for boring after the kind of Christmas vacation I had. For an article about Mueller Sports Medicine bottles, I call half the sporting goods store owners in Texas.

all their names are buhba, I text Glen, though when he'd texted me *goodmorning star eyes,* I promised myself I wouldn't reply. Amid my coworkers I feel glassy-eyed and ill at ease; to be in the company of so many purposeful adults nauseates me. It doesn't help that people keep asking how I enjoyed my holiday. Did I ski at Sugarbush? I did not, but the name of the resort makes me blush.

All day the texts roll in, arriving at fifty-minute intervals that I figure out must be the passing period between classes. He is reluctantly doing calculus; he is eating Fritos at 11:00 a.m. while dissecting a mink; now he's watching a concentration-camp film in which Jewish prisoners dig holes into which they will be pushed by their comrades once the SS shoots them. *what a day*, he texts at three, and while I'm not sure whether to read his tone as earnest or sarcastic, I'm struck by the strangeness and savagery of high school. Where else do you dissect minks and watch death-camp footage in the course of a single day? Even a decade later, I still feel visceral hate and fear toward high school, where I did not fit in and was sometimes subjected to taunts and small humiliations. I wonder if this is what life is like for Glen, in his blazers and suede boots. He has so much more confidence than I did when I was his age; his knowledge and enthusiasms keep him company. I wanted so much to conform that I banished enthusiasms, lest they get me singled out. I wouldn't have been caught dead carrying around an e. e. cummings book.

Only a few people text me on a regular basis, and my father is one of them. I think the brevity appeals to him. Often he begins his texts with "hey kid." I wonder if he thinks of Dawn's kids as his kids too, or if they're bracketed in some way that only allows him to have step-feelings for them. My dad and Dawn want to drive into Queens this weekend to try a new Asian fusion restaurant Dawn read about in *Newsday*. Would I like to come?

Another message dings through.

we might bring the boys

I think about how my father thinks of Glen as a boy. If he knew I had sex with Glen, would he think of me as a pedophile, a sicko? I have never discussed any of my sexual partners with my father, but Glen exists in a whole other category. I imagine my father and Dawn never speaking to me again, my being banished from our blended family. Maybe Glen and I could run away together and live on an island of some sort. Not Long Island. Bora Bora? I see that I'm not thinking rationally. My phone dings again.

had to masturbate thinking about you hope you don't mind me saying. long day w/o you.

He misses me, and I miss him, too. We're locked in this. When I get home from work I lie facedown on the sofa, picturing him and his elegant hands and his tics until I come. Usually I don't feel shame after

I masturbate, but this time I feel an awful leaden ball in my stomach, and I vow never to think about Glen in a sexual context again. I write it down in my notebook: *I will never think about Glen in a sexual context again.* It helps to commit my vow to paper.

❧

Glen calls that night, and we talk about an essay he has to write about Ibsen's *A Doll's House*, which he finds insipid even though he knows it was groundbreaking in its time. We go on about Torvald and Nora for a while, but I'm distracted by the Asian fusion restaurant plans my father suggested.

"I like how he calls her 'my poor little sweet-tooth.' Like she's not good for him but he loves her anyway," Glen says.

I see this as an opening and tell him he shouldn't come with my father and Dawn this weekend. "It'll be too weird. They'll be able to tell about us."

"I won't let on anything," he says. "I'm capable of being completely normal."

Okay, I say. I'll go to the restaurant with my father and his fiancée and my stepbrothers. And I'll believe a seventeen-year-old with Tourette's when he promises he'll act normal.

I meet them at Tangra, in Sunnyside, a few stops on the 7 train from my apartment. My father and Dawn are ebullient, happily almost hitched. Greg's at a sleepover but Garrett, the youngest, seems to have gotten sartorial advice from Glen. He's wearing a blazer with a white oxford-cloth shirt and dress pants, like a mini Glen, though with Converse sneakers instead of suede boots. Garrett bears enough resemblance to Glen that I feel my stomach start to roil. As bad as it is that I've taken up with Glen, what if I'd preyed on Garrett? Is being attracted to my father's stepchildren catalogued in the *DSM*?

We sit down at a round table under hanging red pagoda mobiles. There are huge vases of silk flowers all around. I end up between Dawn and Garrett, with my father and Glen across from me. I'm acutely disappointed to be so far from Glen. His hair is still damp. An ellipsis of acne trails down the left side of his face.

We talk fusion cuisine. We debate the merits of poached tofu, of fried nori chips, of Sonoma foie gras yakiniku, of jicama something-or-other with hijiki. My father and Dawn let Glen drink a glass of wine, but I'm too nervous to drink any more than the coffee cup of jug wine I gulped on the way over, fearful that I'll slip up, let my feelings show (whatever my feelings are; I'm wandering in the vast abyss composed of equal parts love, shame, fear, self-loathing, and lust), reveal that I have very much enjoyed sucking my stepbrother's cock of late and, worse, have enjoyed even more having him go down on me. In short, while tackling my plate of jicama hijiki with splintery chopsticks, I realize I've had a sexual awakening these past few weeks, and as I take small sips of wine (small sips!), I begin to see that I'm not willing to give that up. I'm astonished by this dapper person across from me in his wool blazer and white button-down inking diagrams of proscenia on the paper table cover and explaining his set design for a play written by his friend Rob. Acne ellipsis be damned, this is a person who can whip up a pureed soup from some old butternut squash I couldn't get inspired to do anything about, a person who knows all the words to "Minnie the Moocher" and, in addition, that "kick the gong around" in said song is a reference to opium use. I see as if looking back from a time long in the future that Glen's going to be a great artist, musician, an entertainer and scholar, a public intellectual on the order of Susan Sontag or Cornel West, both of whom he's read. Am I going to deny myself this greatness because he's seventeen and my stepbrother? Or am I going to put these irrelevancies aside and start living my big life?

"Are you okay?" Dawn asks. Everyone is looking at me. Tears keep spilling out of my eyes.

I don't know what to say. I'm not okay. I'm happier and sadder and more worried than I've ever been.

"Hard week at work?" my father asks.

I still can't speak. My eyes keep leaking of their own accord. "I'll take her for a walk," Glen says. "We'll get her a little air." Dawn says that's a good idea. I grab my purse.

Outside, we stand in front of a costume and wig shop that's still open.

"Let's get some," he says. "We can be anyone." I'm crying harder now.

"I know," he says.

I know he knows.

I will be Jimi Hendrix. He'll be Lincoln. I'll be the princess of a small, ineffectual monarchy. He'll be a telephone line repairman. I'll be red-headed. He'll have dreadlocks.

We walk. We walk. We keep walking, until everything catches up with us.

BodSwap™ with Moses

Manuela in scrubs top and cheetah pants hasn't even finished telling us what to expect from our new bodies when the Kenyans stride in on their excellent legs. She shouts each of their names. "Kipchoge! Nourreddine! Alpesh!" She looks down at her clipboard again like maybe it's lying. "Moses?"

These are the Kenyan runners who didn't make the cut. Didn't win the Boston Marathon, didn't win New York, didn't even win the Caballeros de Yuma or the Chinklacamoose Marathon. Maybe they came in seventh. Maybe they tore a hamstring and hopped off the course in excruciating pain at the eighteen-mile marker. Maybe they had diarrhea running down their leg that day and the Americans for once beat them. The way Manuela talks, you'd think these Kenyans couldn't do twenty-six miles in a station wagon. In elite sports you need to be elite to compete, Manuela says. If you're not elite you're salt, and not the good kind of Himalayan pink salt sold at the finer supermarket chains but the salt poured on the street after a blizzard. Road salt.

Manuela hates they took her out of PICU and stuck her in Bariatrics. Her motto is Bariatrics es como Prohibition: a really bad idea. On days she's feeling cruddy, Bariatrics es como the Holocaust: a really really bad idea. I've tried to learn some Spanish from Manuela, as the sound of her first language puts her in a better mood. Results: mixed.

Now Manuela yells our names. "Donna! Patti! Tish! Gretchen! Bertha!"

We are the fat ladies in the post-post-post-post-Obamacare circus that is healthcare in America. We are the lackers of self-control who snack on Turfshaker bars that weigh three pounds each. I have tried every weight-loss scheme in the book. I tried la tummy tuck and la lapband y la stomach staple y el biliopancreatic diversion con duodenal switch. At one point I considered having todo el estomago removed. Now I'm down to the last option: BodSwap™ with one of these washed-up Kenyans. Manuela's other motto is "Kenyans Melt the Fat Away, Okay Okay." Because they do. And then they give us our bodies back. Like dry cleaning.

We sit in red plastic chairs made for dwarf children, and the Kenyans rotate from one fat lady to the next. My first is Kipchoge. He has a huge forehead. He's a member of a Bantu tribe. Bantu are foraging peoples. I tell him I'm the opposite of a foraging people, unless foraging means digging around in the freezer at night for another Turfshaker bar. I spend two minutes talking about the 1.5-pound Turfshaker versus the new and much-touted Turfshaker with double the Chewy High Calorie Fun. He tells me his parents died in a cholera epidemic, plus all nine siblings were killed by invading tribes.

Moses bouncing on the edge of his plastic chair has a wary look of emergency, like he might make a break for it. Well, he won't be doing much of that if he ends up BodSwapping with me. He has a disorder so his hands shake. We're all damaged goods, but he's a little more than most. It occurs to me I might be able to negotiate a discount if I Bod-Swap™ with him.

Moses asks me how I got so big. I tell Moses: Baby, I was born big.

Moses asks if largeness maybe also has anything to do with the America food that is so fast.

I tell Moses genetics is a bummer.

Moses agrees many things a bummer, such as civil war in his country and also cholera epidemic.

I'm not sure I'm so crazy about Moses, even if I were to get the shaky-hands discount. Moses is judgy.

Our three minutes are up.

Nourreddine asks me to stand up and turn in a circle.

No one who weighs 350 pounds wants to turn in a circle. "Please, I help you with my lonely determination." Nourreddine has a good attitude and wolfish teeth. Before this he trained in Tokyo, where he was the tallest person in the city and no one spoke to him for four years.

Nourreddine tells me about the tribal markings on his face. I show him the dolphin tattoo on my wrist. Once I'm skinny I plan to get three more dolphins leaping over a rainbow on my lower back.

He makes approving noises. "If I had the tattoo it would be the tattoo of your face right here." He points to his chest.

Wow, over-the-top. But okay. Sell it, Nourreddine.

🦪

I wake from surgery with Elise's hands on my face. "Keep your hands under the sheet," she whispers.

"Stop smushing my face."

"I'm *caressing* your face. That's what a lover's hands do."

"It feels like smushing." Elise and I have been together nine years. She's a late-to-the-party lesbian and very *attached*. If she could attach herself to me so the two of us merged into one big double-vaginaed, Turfshaker-bar-eating body, she would put up the money in an instant.

"Eventually you're gonna wanna hold hands, my love. May as well embrace the darkness."

"Don't say it that way," Elise says priggishly.

I decide now's not the time to tell her I went in for the Moses Shaky Hands Discount.

Elise was married to a man before we got together, so the temporary Kenyan penis thing shouldn't be a big deal. The bigger deal is the temporary Kenyan black skin thing. Elise didn't grow up around blacks and says they makes her nervous. "Believe you me, Sugar Magnolia," I told her, "your skin, historically speaking, should rightfully make them far nervouser than theirs makes you."

A few days later I wake up with a huge thing for the supermodel

Iman. And by "thing," I mean an ill-concealed-from-Manuela-who's-checking-my-vitals hard-on. Iman in tiny leatherette shorts, Iman with gold-dipped feather earrings and a gold bra, Iman crawling toward me on her knees with her purple-black aureoles pushing in my direction, and boy is my mouth open and drooling in anticipation. Yeezus, are porno Iman fantasies how Moses gets through a marathon?

"Hey, Mama," I say, not knowing that many Kenyans refer to women generally in greeting as "Mama."

"I'll bend that thing till it breaks off you." Manuela actually swipes at it, like the penis tenting the sheets is a species of rodent.

"Don't mess with the merchandise. I gotta give it back," I remind her.

Look at how those cheetah pants flatter the buxomness of Manuela's lower half. Even her scrubs top with the miniature deer-galloping-away-from-hunters-blasting-at-them-with-rifles pattern gets me going.

So this is what it's like to be a man from the neck down. Everything activates me.

I'm like a horndog version of Elise's immune system in hay fever season.

When finally I get home from the hospital our little dog Jean-Charles decides she doesn't know me, or at least doesn't like the person with my face and Moses's shaky black hands to pet her. Hadn't anticipated that; also hadn't anticipated Elise walking so slowly because of her rheumatoid arthritis that I end up carrying her back from walking the dog, though since the dog won't let me carry her as well, Elise slung over my shoulder has to hold the leash while the dog and I make our way around the golf course in the middle of our development. I'm starting to like these Kenyan legs.

"All the blood's rushing to my head," Elise complains. She's kind of big to stay hoisted over my shoulder. I think about the weird sensation of all the blood rushing to Moses's cock whenever I think about Iman or even Manuela. Beezus, Manuela in those cheetah pants! I bet she's a monster in the sack. I force myself to stop thinking about Manuela in the sack and wonder how Moses is doing with all 350 pounds of me attached to him. It occurs to me I should call the guy, ask him to coffee, give him the last seventeen Turfshaker bars from the freezer if he's got cravings, ask him the names of the foods I've been craving, maybe or maybe not mention Iman.

It's a while before we're able to meet at the Moonduck's in the strip mall near the hospital. I wonder if I'll recognize myself or if Moses will have slimmed me down beyond recognition. The quid pro quo for these Kenyans getting citizenship is they've got to MELTFATFAST™, and that means getting our big bodies up and running as soon as the sutures heal.

I spot Moses in a corner of the shop. He looks schlumpier than I remember.

Right, of course, that's because he's carrying around a couple hundred extra pounds. He's got my body wearing a lavender (not my color) T-shirt with the sleeves cut off and the word *Jazzercise!* on the chest. Cheezus, if there's one thing I don't miss it's my ample and not particularly well-defined bosom. It's like a single entity that reaches from just below the neck to somewhere in the vicinity of his waist. My waist. Whatever.

"How you been, Mama?" he asks.

"What's happening, Bro? You going to Jazzercise?"

"Two or three times in a day. Your body cannot run yet, so we dance. Dancing melts the fat and puts the joy in your overwork heart."

My heart? I'm getting confused about personal pronouns. Does this mean I tell him he's having a lot of joy in his overwork penis? About Iman fantasies and even some about Manuela our bariatric nurse? "I always liked to dance," I say, deciding prudence is the better part of valor. "I mean, you know, swaying to the beat of 'Ebony and Ivory' kind of thing."

"Not aerobic dancing like to the beat of Outkast 'Hey Ya'?"

I admit I have never aerobic-danced to "Hey Ya." Not even close.

Moses sips a black coffee, and I slurp at something frappuccinized topped with whipped duck fat.

"Shake it like the Polaroid picture," Moses says as I lick cream off my lip. The deal is I'm allowed to do whatever I want with his body, but his job with mine is to MELTFATFAST™. I didn't ask to be born a fat American with cash any more than Moses put in for cholera epidemics and tribal warfare. You take what's handed to you.

"My hands still shaking?" Moses asks. "I like your hands." He holds them out for me and they feel like they're old friends I haven't seen in a while. "Your hands don't shake, and they both have cushions."

"My hands are pudgy."

"Pudgy," he says slowly.

"You have strong hands, even though they do shake."

He shakes his head wistfully. "I get strong hands in the wars. We use the bow and arrow."

"In the twenty-first century you use a bow and arrow?"

"Maasai tradition."

"Kreezus." I put my frothy drink down and hold out his big strong hands to clasp my small pudgy ones that look like fat white fish that can dart away invisible under the sea grass. "Buddy, you need some new traditions."

Moses nods gravely. "Bow and arrow more deadly than machete."

"Did you kill people with a machete, too?" I look at the black hands with their ropy veins on the backs. All these hands have been doing recently is knitting a freaking balaclava for the neighbor's kid.

Moses starts to tell me more about machetes, but I stop him. I'm not sure I want to hear about these hands taking human life via bow and arrow, machete, or whatever other vintage killing tool is in the offing.

Who is Moses anymore and who am I? I am not a person who would kill anyone with a machete, even the worst possible rapist with a long rap sheet. If Moses got sent back to Kenya right now, would he try to kill one of those rival tribe guys with my pudgy hands? I think of how Elise still won't hold my hand unless I grab hers, and then her hand gets all sweaty and she makes me let go.

"Moses, I have something to ask you."

"Ask."

"What if we didn't swap back yet?"

He looks startled. "Isn't it the rules?"

"What if I went and talked to them? I could pay extra or something."

Moses nods without speaking. Is there any more American phrase than "I could pay extra or something"?

I whisper when I tell Moses the reason: how my partner of nine years wakes me now in the dark of our bed at night and nuzzles my face with her chin and tells me she wants me to hold her down and do it to her. *Give it to me,* she whispers in my ear, *with that big strong cock.*

"Things are going well for you and my . . . body," Moses says. I concede this. Things are going spiffily.

"Your wife likes when you're a man for her."

"Something like that."

Moses smiles.

"What about your wife?" I ask.

"'A woman's polite devotion is her greatest beauty.' African proverb."

"So it's cool?" No one can say I don't look the image of suave in this tracksuit. In my old life I would have killed to look this good. "I can keep you for a while?" I feel like I'm talking about an adoptable pug.

"We enjoy your hands," Moses says. "We find uses for them." He offers a mischievous grin.

"Not bow and arrow?" I say.

"Or machete. Soft hands."

We shimmy together, a little Jazzercise move I remember from the old days, when I couldn't lose the weight and Elise rejected me. "You'll be okay?" I ask. He gives a little ceremonial bow, and I almost say hi to myself in that lavender shirt. *Hi, self.* As I pull onto the highway, I see Moses on the dusty service road, walking my body down to size.

Omaha

He wanted to speak to her. There was a storefront on their block he
hadn't noticed, and then one day it sprung itself on him: Claddagh Elec-
tronics. This confounded him, both that he had not noticed and the
conjoining of the two words. He took it as an omen. There were days
he still could not believe he lived in Queens now. The skyline across the
river shocked him. He would tell her that: "Sometimes I jump back, as if
it's going to fall on me, like a façade." No. He could never say "façade." It
was how he felt, but sounded like something he'd read. Above all things
he didn't want to seem to her artificial or on the make.

There was an Irish bar down the street, on the avenue perpendicular.
Irish, but. The girls who worked there were all from Armagh. Sometimes he had arguments with them. It occurred to ask them about the
woman with the dog.

"Her?" They thought he was having them on. He could not formulate
why—whether it was that she was an American, or whether the problem
lay somehow in him.

The one named Kay looked at the ceiling when he pressed her. No, it
wasn't something she'd thought about. He had just caught her off guard

with a notion like that, was all. "It's like she's just sort of Bohemian," she said at last.

Also probably a Jew. He got that later, from the one named Fiona. They weren't sure they could put their finger on it.

He took to watching her through the blind slats. Her dog wasn't one recognizable breed, but a mixture of common ones, glossy black with comical tufts of white on the backs of its hind legs. It struggled valiantly against a contraption she hooked over its snout. Did the contraption have to do with her being American or this being a city or neither of these? In Navan the dogs weren't kept on leads; it would have been seen as an affectation. There had been one eccentric who fashioned a lead out of pieces of belts and suspenders. But this was understood as a dimension of an affliction.

He worked for a package delivery company. Some days he made deliveries and others he stayed at dispatch and loaded or unloaded. He was required to wear a brace for support. It looped over his shoulders and crisscrossed in the middle of his back. He had an instinct this would be something to which she would object. Not in principle, but the look of it. He didn't want her to see him in his uniform.

One day they met in the shop at the end of the street. He had noticed the dog tied to a parking meter in front. She was already at the counter when he went in. It was not in his character to study or interpret anyone's purchases; she was the one who remarked and blushed. A roll of toilet paper, something white in a jar like mayonnaise only whiter, pantyhose in a package with a woman in a top and no bottoms, just hose. So what? He smiled and shrugged at her. He had not known the store sold pantyhose. It was a Qwik Mart owned by Arabs. They smoked in the store. Whichever of them was on the register always smoked and had the phone to his ear. He admired that. It was off-putting, but he admired it. He himself lived in this country so tentatively. As if any day someone might come and cuff him or shuttle him off to the airport.

"I want to ask you something," he said.

"Okay." She went outside to wait with the dog. He realized she believed he had come inside to shop.

He grabbed off the shelves the first things he saw. Vienna sausages in a can. Something called Funny Bones, a filled chocolate dessert. Filled with what, he couldn't tell. American food was baffling.

He had to ask the Arab for the cigarettes; his brand wasn't out on display. The Arab looked perturbed and got tangled in the phone cord while searching for the carton.

She was talking to the dog outside. He tried to keep his tread light.

"You have no idea what I'm saying, but you'll be so excited when you see them!" She was hugging the dog's neck and calling it Roach.

Now he made a noise so she would hear him. "Is your dog called Roach?"

The woman's grin was exasperated. "She already knew her name when I got her." She beamed up at him from where she was kneeling. "Are you Irish? No, British? No, Irish."

"Irish."

"That's fantastic."

What about it might she consider fantastic?

"And you're living over here."

"For the time being." He had a premonition she was going to ask why and that he wouldn't be able to prevent himself from badmouthing home with the same tired remark: *Last one out turn off the lights.* It was 1988. Everyone was very doom-and-gloom about Ireland. He was in desperate need of another tack. Not because he felt bad about saying it but because it was boring.

He asked, "What sort of a dog is that?"

"Multiple breeds. No one knows."

"The noise doesn't bother him?"

"She's always been a city dog."

He wanted to see her apartment. It would give a better idea of how far off the mark he was. In his conduct and whatnot. She untied the dog from the meter and invited him with a gesture to walk with her.

"You live up this way, too. Right?"

"I do." He wondered whether she knew which apartment was his.

The dog all of a sudden went crazy, flailing and flopping at the end of the lead like a caught fish. Someone had thrown two sirloin steaks in the street. This was in front of a restaurant reputed to be Mafia-owned, Mafia-patronized, Mafia, Mafia, Mafia.

"I'm so tired of hearing about it," she said. "I mean it's not like they *do* anything, and they take care of the neighborhood. Those geraniums in the hanging pots are theirs."

He had not believed what people said. But sirloins in the street seemed somehow to confirm it. A capacity for lavish wastefulness. An elderly man in a hat and galoshes was poking one with the tip of his umbrella.

It occurred to him to be heroic. He dashed over and picked up the steaks and then went and disposed of them. In his hands they felt like things that knew they were being handled.

She was waiting when he got back, the dog sitting obediently at her feet.

"And they told us the streets would be paved with gold," he said.

She laughed. She was a beautiful laugher.

"And you're funny," she said. It was said in the spirit of discovery. They were both still laughing, but then she abruptly shut her mouth and pulled at the dog's lead.

And you're funny. He would spend a lot of time on that later.

At her stoop she asked if he would like to come in. She was planning on making something in her wok; maybe he would like some of it.

"Now what sort of a thing would you make in a wok?" he said as they climbed the stairs. He was behind her and the dog was in front, its claws scrabbling. He had a brief fright when he saw his own hand going out to touch her pants. They were made of some diaphanous lavender material that almost seemed porous. As if he could put his hand through it and there would be his hand on her skin.

"You could do anything," she was saying. "Only I don't do chicken or any of the other meats."

"You're a vegetarian, then."

She unlocked her door and leaned to turn on a lamp. Her face was apologetic. "Vegetarian, blah blah," she said. "Batiked raiments, paper not plastic."

He got it. "You're bored with yourself."

"Not so much with myself as with my quote lifestyle."

Her apartment was not spectacular. There was not even a TV. But she had things of interest: a book about Houdini, a book of large photographs of what she described as consumer landscapes (a landfill, a junkyard, miles of resort beaches), small sculptures made of rusted metal, handmade wooden boxes with things inside she'd collected: fortune cookie slips, comics from chewing gum wrappers, notes friends had sent her, clippings from newspapers all over the country. There was an item from a paper in Greenville, New York:

July 12: Police received a report of a dog with a chicken in its mouth on River Street at 10:18 a.m. Police found the dog, but there was no chicken.

He wasn't sure why you'd clip a thing like that.

"I don't know," she said. Then: "It's just funny. That they would go to the trouble of putting it in the paper."

"Not too much goes on in some places," he said.

She had begun chopping carrots. Behind the amusement over the clipping he sensed some broader, more encompassing criticism of small-town life. He had grown up in a house without a telephone. Even when it was possible to get one inexpensively, his mother had refused. His mother had been a monumental drunk, but cunning and deft about it. Hiding her conduct but also the bottles. She would put them in the back of the linen press, and once a week or so he would take them out of the house in an old pillow sham. They never spoke about it. Now she was dead. For the way she'd handled herself, he was grateful to her. So few people had known—maybe in the end only his father and him.

"And besides," he said, "how would they know they had the right dog if it didn't have the chicken?"

He was trying to inject levity, but she had already moved on. "Do you want some wine?" She turned to him from her cutting board. She had put on an apron, black and white. He was distracted by the floating implements printed on it: spatula, tongs, pots and pans, a long piercing fork he didn't have a name for.

"I don't drink wine." As soon as he said it, he realized there was no need to be completely honest regarding every single thing about himself.

"Do you drink?" She looked for an instant mildly alarmed.

"Oh I drink. I drink. I do drink."

She was laughing again now, so he didn't mind that he sounded like a skipping record.

She got him a bottle of beer out of the refrigerator. When she gave it to him she went up on her toes and kissed the side of his face, near his ear. "Oh," she said and went quickly back to the cutting board. "I did not think I was going to do that."

The dog was sprawled across the threshold between the kitchen and living room.

She slapped her palms twice on the fronts of her thighs. "Did you?"

🐕

They dated all that spring and summer, going to each other's apartments on weekends or after work. Sometimes she agitated to go to the neighborhood's Irish bar. He felt she was only doing so because she thought he wanted to. He didn't know how to tell her it was really an Armagh bar, not his people. She thought all Irish were his people; the gradations weren't visible to her. So sometimes they went. In any case there was stout on tap and a jukebox that played U2 and a culchie band he liked, the Saw Doctors.

"What's culchie?"

He was not in general as good at explaining things as she was. A pity, because she asked often.

"Culchie's sort of like, well." He was stuck. Then he got it. "Like in the town with the dog with the chicken in its mouth."

That delighted her. She wanted immediately to hear more.

"Well, for instance that song 'Hay Wrap.' The chorus is what the lads shout while they're working."

She wouldn't let it go at that.

"When they're baling hay. And then the rhythm of the song is like the rhythm of the baling machine."

She was looking at him warmly as he spoke. She picked a piece of lint off his shirt. Even that was done warmly, as if he were a great man preparing to give a lecture and she was the one charged with shining him up beforehand. "See, what you're doing there is a version of sociology," she said.

"What I'm doing is talking a lot of shite."

She was an adjunct professor at City College. He had not so much transcended his embarrassment at his ignorance of *sociology* as he had reluctantly given in to it. Now, with a beer or two in him, he tackled *adjunct*.

"There's no job for me. Not full-time." They were walking from the bar to the Vernon-Jackson subway station. "I could move to Kansas or Nebraska for a full-time job tomorrow practically, but I don't want to."

She was taking him to the Angelika. He didn't know what the Angelika was exactly, but he assumed it had to be a movie house of some sort. She had taken him to a museum where they screened movies, and everyone there had been dressed in black and the wire-rimmed glasses people who wore black often wore. A trick he played to calm down when there was a surplus of things he didn't know was to imagine outlandish possibilities. For instance, maybe the Angelika would be a brothel floating on the Hudson River. Often with her he found himself in situations among people far more educated than he. Once it was a University Club where everyone had a Ph.D. and was drinking martinis. The whole evening seemed to be people gliding around and nodding. It was excruciating only because he had not adequately prepared his mind. He had thought from the name that the University Club would be maybe a bar with kegs and pretzels and sawdust on the floor. Instead it had been plush carpeting and leather upholstery gleaming from all the corners, dim lamps with green glass shades like the lamps at a law office, the gliding and nodding, the quiet.

The trick was to identify in advance a range of possibilities. Then no matter what he was hit with, he could catch it and punt.

❧

Then it was her turn to be amazed. One Sunday morning in late September he took her in the other direction on the subway, farther out in Queens. The Breffni was the name of the place, in Sunnyside.

"This is a Meath pub." He was going to expire with pleasure, like a child confronting the wrapping paper and tangle of ribbons preventing him from getting at the gift inside.

The pub was almost inhumanly packed. This was at 9:00 a.m. Several parties at the bar were wolfing down piles of bacon and eggs, scraping the lasts with triangles of toast. Beer was being served in sweating pint glasses and handed over people's heads.

She became a fount of questions; they just spun out as if they had been folded up inside her all her life. He would be trying to explain something, and she would not be able to keep herself from breaking in with another question.

He insisted on paying for everything they drank. He seemed taller; people knew him.

He had a nickname.

"What's a Knacker? What's Knacker?"

All at once everyone stood and began gently to sing. The way the mood went in an instant from profane to sacred gripped her. It was the national anthem, but *their* national anthem. She didn't know a word of it or even the language. Then they went right back again, as if a switch had been flipped. "Ah, ye cunt ye," someone said. She turned to see the direction it came from. It was about a bet.

He was signaling the bartender. "Same again," he said. Then to her: "Why don't you get out your pencil and notebook?"

He was at his leisure. He was not to be commanded like her tufted dog. She looked down at her shoes, open-toed sandals. Already her toes were washed in beer. Her attempts were always so far off the mark. She had in fact brought her notebook, but probably unconsciously, and deliberately had neglected to bring a writing implement. She was very particular and favored one brand of mechanical pencil.

"Look at me," he said.

She raised her head.

"I'm just funnin' you. I love your pencils." He was beaming. As if he was waiting for her to write a whole textbook about it, right down to the triangles of toast.

"I had a dream you left me," she said. Instantly she hated herself for the nakedness of the confession.

He took her up in his arms, so that she was lifted off her stool. "I had a dream I hooked you in."

He was wearing the green-and-yellow jersey of his team. It smelled new, like plastic and rubber.

❦

She mentioned to her family that she loved the way he smelled. No good came of it. She had two younger sisters, both married to men they'd met in college. It was transparent to everyone that she was rebelling. She had metamorphosed from a most practical person into someone fuzzy-eyed. No, that wasn't true. There had always been seeds of it, in the boxes she kept with the fortunes and clippings and comics. She had been waiting all her life to be one of the people who values the little filaments over the grand arc. Now it had happened.

"*Smelled* doesn't put a down payment on a house," her father said.

"I don't want a house."

The grand arc didn't interest her at all anymore.

"Smelled doesn't take care of you in your dotage," her mother said.

They were sitting on her parents' porch. Long Island. It was almost too late in the season to sit outside, but they were stoic in fleece. She could hear a dog barking in the distance. She thought of her own, asleep by herself in Queens on the little green bed like a lozenge. That dog was the underlying melody of her whole life. The only constant, the invariable factor or whatever it was called in math. With him she was a woman with a dog. So also with her family.

"In my dotage I want to be taken out and shot."

"Well," her mother said. She seemed on the verge of amplifying, but stopped short. Her family gave a lot of credence to the idea that the Irish were violent. Violence as a feature of character rather than a response to circumstances. Oh, they had a hundred examples. It became something of a family activity when they got together, like jigsaw puzzles or talking about the Kennedys.

Someone was chewing ice. You could hear the sound of it sparking against teeth.

"That's not fair," she said. Violence had been done to the Kennedys. They weren't the doers.

"Oh, they were doers all right," her father said. He voted Republican. Everyone knew he was being unfair. But families are often unfair. They are amoeboid in character, looking only to engulf.

࿒

She grew away from them. She grew away like a plant grows away from shadow. Or those were the terms in which she thought about it. When she talked with other adjuncts over soup and crackers she made an effort to sound as if the growing away was inevitable, Irishman or no. It was the college cafeteria, but she had gotten the rest of them to start calling it the Cantina. His influence. A certain zing. He called the garbage *rubbage* and the two hours on Sunday morning he spent preventing her from getting out of bed *the ecstaticals.*

One of the women stood up suddenly. She looked as if she was going to overturn her bowl of soup.

"Are we just supposed to stay here and be adjuncts forever?"

She herself felt calm. She didn't even put down her spoon.

"We can leave anytime we want."

"Go to Nebraska."

The example was always Nebraska.

"We should unionize," one said. But she was new and always having ideas.

The standing woman clenched her fists up near her face. She was wearing a taupe jacket with a Happy Thanksgiving button on her lapel. It was shaped like a Puritan's hat.

"What am I doing with my life?" she said.

No one said anything. She kept standing there.

"Thanksgiving's in three days, señorita."

She sat down. Her eyes were wet.

࿒

They were lying on his bed. It was only a twin; his outer arm hung off the side. She told him about the woman and her outburst over soup. She meant for the point of the story to be how calm she'd been. But it went into something else.

Her problem was she didn't want enough. In this, he said, she would fit in well with the people back home.

Yeats was from Ireland, she said. Yeats had wanted all sorts of things.

"But abstract things, truth and love and a united Ireland." He was thinking of the people back home in Navan. He wondered what abstract things his mother had wanted. The only thing she'd ever asked for was bottle of Jameson's and then the next. And then of course getting rid of the bottles. A negative getting. He had never mentioned this, not wanting to seem like a case. Sociologists like cases.

He talked more like she did now, used words like "abstract."

She had never told him about her family, their scathing pronouncements. The excuse she made to herself was not wanting to hurt his feelings. This overlooked of course her own. It is taxing to love someone a great deal and at the same time know that no one in your family is rooting for you.

"Maybe you should try to advance yourself in your career," he said.

He might have been reading the line out of an instruction book.

She sat up on the bed. "You know I'm happy this way. Why would you suggest something like that?"

She stood in his bathroom. She didn't have to go but needed a moment. Omaha. The word just hung, in thin bright letters. She didn't blink it away. The toilet paper from the Arabs' store reeked of cigarette smoke. There was another, unopened roll stashed up high. She took it out of the bathroom with her and made him smell it. She was often intractable when it came to small things. Righting the infinitesimal wrong.

"Please. I'll use it. I'll use it when you're not around."

She was careful not to let her expression change. That wasn't the point, she said.

He knew that wasn't the point, but the smell wouldn't make them waive their no-returns policy. "They're whores for the smoking," he observed pragmatically.

"It's not fair," she said. "It's disgusting."

"Those are two separate issues."

Before, nothing was an issue. Now toilet paper was.

There's a recurring dream she has. No, not so much even a dream—it comes to her unbidden while she's awake. But she associates "daydream" with fantasies, hopes, wishes. This is not a hope or wish.

She would be sitting on the floor of her apartment with the dog beside her, its head in her lap. Out of nowhere she would think, I could take my fist and smash it down on this head. I could hold the jaw shut, get a knife and stab its flank full of holes. Then the dog would be screaming, if dogs scream. At a certain point it would go quiet and die, and she would dispose of its body in a dumpster. There was a giant one alongside the Mafia restaurant.

This was such a horrible thought, and so outside or beyond anything she would ever want or be capable of that she felt sick with herself. Like she didn't want to be herself. She would have to be somebody else or dead.

"Do dogs scream?" she asked. She told him about her dream.

In the morning, his mother would fix the tea with milk and pour it into an empty whiskey bottle and wrap it in a cloth for him to take to school.

He thought of telling that. A car alarm went off. Then another.

"Well," he said.

How there had been no such thing as a thermos. How there was in the tea a lingering smell. Ferment. How he would drink it in the lane beside his house and stow the bottle in the stones for the walk home.

He would come in the back door from school. That door was always propped open, rain or shine. Silence. He would begin to prepare himself to find her. The catechism already needling through his head. A small, strangled sound. Not death—not a scream at all. It resolved itself into the sound of his name. She would only want him to get her a glass of water, the pack of cigarettes she'd misplaced, a light.

Restraint

There's a certain kind of war veteran who refuses to talk about his past. His face is still handsome but hard as chrome. When he was younger he had upright posture, a handsome man's confidence. His marriage has defeated him. His home is a restored Victorian, quiet as a museum. A Volvo station wagon in the driveway, its seats worn smooth. "When I die they'll bury me with this car," he says. His wife has always been less attractive than he. She's dowdy, and now the gray shows through the auburn.

He has been walking his dog and listening to public radio through headphones. Now he feels her eyes on him. She looks as if she has been jogging. Her ash-blond hair is held back in a loose braid. She's still catching her breath.

He says his wife is out of town for a pastel conference. She pictures women in Easter dresses.

"Art classes," he says.

They walk the long blocks to his house, and he puts the dog inside. "Do you want to go for a ride?" he asks.

"Won't someone see us?" She has never been in a car with him.

He hands her his newspaper. "Hold this up like you're reading."

He drives slowly through the town, his hand on her leg. There's an advertisement for Yellow Box shoes. She thinks of two feet with yellow boxes on them.

They married after the war. She sent him letters when he was stationed in Hanoi.

Why did he marry her? He shrugs. Why does anyone do anything? It was something about that time after the war.

"You mean the war messed you up?"

"The war made it—the war shifted the meaning of everything."

"How?" He has missed spots shaving. She would like to groom him, soap his chin and guide the razor down the planes of his face.

"Nothing in my life matters more than the time I was at war." It's an effort to get this out. "Nothing mattered after."

He did not have children. He did not have love, he said, though he had been married for decades. It was understood he wouldn't divorce. She couldn't fathom why. A fellow law student had introduced her to him at a hog roast. It was not what you would expect. Champagne flutes, a jazz trio, canapés.

"I wish we could go to a bar." She knows she sounds plaintive. He stares straight ahead. His hand wanders up her thigh.

"The Vieux Carré? Behind the sick mall."

"What do you mean sick mall?"

"The one near Wal-Mart. There's a bar around back."

"Isn't it a dump?"

"That's its charm."

Two o'clock. The drunks are just getting settled. On the jukebox a song she remembers from her childhood, her parents dancing in their work clothes. His hand rests on the back of her neck. Her eyes struggle to adjust. Outside it had been so bright.

"I would advise against the wine."

"Vodka?"

He gets two vodka sodas with lime. They come in plastic cups loaded with ice chips. The vodka tastes strong and bad.

"Not top shelf," he says.

An afternoon passes, an era. He uses the word "daren't." His favorite book is *Justine*. She has never heard of it. In a way this offends him.

"I have gone over every inch of you," he says. Now her eyes have adjusted. He has one tooth that slightly overlaps the one next to it. "Then I did it again, to make sure I had fully explored you."

The man next to them gags or dry-heaves.

His name is Pell. He's sixty-three: older than her father. She will berate herself for what she is doing, what is about to happen.

"I would like for us to be together," she says simply. It is not simple. They have finished four vodka sodas between them.

"I don't know how that would ever be."

"I'm not beautiful enough for you. I have too many muscles." She hates herself for the hours on the track, the push-ups. It's not the aesthetic for men his age.

"You are *too* beautiful."

The alcoholic makes his noise again. If only we could score our lives ourselves. One time she remembers being so happy in the supermarket. Then on the loudspeaker came a Muzak version of "Rainy Days and Mondays."

"*Does not everything depend on our interpretation of the silence around us?*"

She stares at him. Her eyes feel heavy in her head like coins. She hopes she hasn't revealed herself completely. He holds all the cards.

"That's a quote. From *Justine.*"

She types the quote into her phone and texts it to herself. The cheerful double chime of her alert. She should be studying for the Georgia bar.

"You're a fucking teenager," he says.

The alcoholic offers his comment. "Kids today!"

They are better than this in bed.

It's almost time. There's heat between them. Angry heat, whatever. She has plans to kiss him roughly, ride him. If she acts like a teenager, so be it. Cherry mint lip gloss, flavored condoms. At the drugstore she hands him the Party Box. "'Crank up the fun with intense flavors and colors.' That's a quote." He swats her fanny. His word. "Daren't." And the way he says the word "temperature": "tem-per-a-toor." Her labia are swelling over a relic. This didn't happen with law-school guys. They did not send her anywhere she couldn't go with a vibrator.

She wanders down two aisles and brings a black plastic comb to the register, where he waits, arms crossed. He has already paid for the Party Box and a bottle of red wine.

"You'll want to," she says. She mouths "afterward." He pays for the comb.

The black guy with tall hair nods smilingly to them as they cross paths at the sliding door.

Everyone must see it, she thinks.

She waits in the car while Pell gets the key from the front desk. He goes in first with the key, and she will follow after two minutes. The Volvo sputters like a lung. Sputter and purr. She likes to think of being in the Volvo as being inside him. She's sitting inside his heart. She is shivering. A maid crosses the lot with new towels stacked on a cart, a spray bottle of disinfectant hung by the trigger. The liquid inside sloshes dark green. Intense flavors and colors. She hopes there's vanilla. But vanilla is not an intense flavor. As if the maid cared, the disinfectant cared. No one in all of Georgia cared. It was a workday. You could feel it like wings beating, all the work getting done. Soon they would be doing their work as well.

The hotel room door opens as if on its own. He always steps behind the door.

More ceremony. Maybe it's military. One time he had her to his house when the wife was away and asked her to take off her shoes. She thought at first his request must be forensic. Shred the evidence. If he killed her he could dispose of the body. Illicit acts, illicit thoughts. They sat in his den and drank bourbon with Coke and lime. Fabulous heavy glassware, made in the last century. One day she would be a real adult, and own things. He had made another request. Would she remove the rest of her clothes? She had chosen a short black skirt with a pink silk blouse and black sandals with tiny pink flowers hand-painted on them from her one time in Spain. All that effort for flowers. She took her time removing each piece and folding it. Then sat with her legs crossed to drink a second bourbon. That her pubic hair was so dark shamed her.

"Look at that pelt." He had pressed his hand just below her belly. Then lifted her in his arms to take her to his bedroom. The wife slept downstairs. Her hand steadied them on the banister as he climbed. She wondered if on the sofa she had left a wet spot.

Now they are in their motel lair. He has removed his expensive shirt. There is red wine in the plastic cups provided. On the television, C-SPAN for the noise.

"God I missed you. I live for you."

She has texted herself these kinds of sentences. The detritus of erotic life is sometimes all you have. He himself does not text. Though he keeps a cell phone in a leather holster.

She will kiss every part of him today; she has promised herself that. The wrinkled skin of his scrotum, and she will run her tongue along the ridges of both his ears. This man with his powerful silver head and all that money will give himself over. His cock is hard in both her hands that she has greased with oil.

"I'm going to climb on you now, okay?" He can't even speak.

They rock against each other, her begging him to thrust.

"Girl, girl," he says at last as she comes, moaning his name. He hangs three fingers in her mouth, reminding her to be quiet.

"I can't, I don't want to." She's crying as if he has fucked a girl, not a woman.

Their bodies go still, both of them startled.

"I'm sorry, I never felt it like that." She bends and licks at his lips, flits her tongue in and out of his mouth. "Oh god oh god," she says.

Now he will get up and make love through the back of her. Her hair, dislodged from the braid, hangs over her face.

"Oh baby girl," he says as he enters her fully. Neither of them cares anymore. This afternoon she is his baby girl. On C-SPAN the senators argue about polar ice caps disappearing.

❦

The most terrible things can happen: the grand summary of his war education.

Elizabeth—this is her name, as it's the name of hundreds of young lovers of older men—Elizabeth does not know, can't even imagine. When you have seen even one terrible thing it is easy to imagine a host of others. When you have experienced the most terrible thing there is a time when you decide you will speak of it or you will agree to silence.

Her name was Bian. He still does not know what her name means. It means secretive, hidden. She came to do the laundry twice a week. While on the base she might spend time with a particular officer. Sergeant Reden was known to favor her. Also Corporal Middie, that asshole. Pell was a Private First Class. Some of the women cared about rank. Bian liked Pell; he was gentle with her. If he planned to approach her he always washed first. You couldn't say that of everyone in the unit. Middie would throw a grenade into a farmer's field just to watch people scatter.

Pell smoked a cigarette; Bian sat on his lap. What eyebrows. *Long may.* He spoke the language poorly but at least tried. He entered her quickly. The great jolt of his one relief from combat. Only in his dreams did he do violence to her.

Middie and Reden didn't like that Bian preferred him.

Why did they care? Reden called all of them gook whores and said he couldn't tell one from another.

Bian told Pell he was her husband. He did not discourage her. When he got an extra cigarette, he put it behind her ear. He put the letters from Ann away as soon as he read through them once. She was studying art at Tulane. She had taken a great interest in bird-watching and found a way to procure field glasses. Scarlet tanager, hermit warbler, vesper sparrow. She might have been writing from the moon to tell him about life on Saturn.

He won money in a card game. Won hooch. Bian refused to go with Middie if Pell wanted her. Middie had a tattoo of a snake on his arm that he told Bian he could make move. She didn't care about any of that. Sometimes she called Pell "Pei." "My Pei." She sat on his lap and smoothed his hair with her hands.

Then things went very bad.

"What did she look like?" Elizabeth asked. They were lying side by side, crosswise on the bed, like they always did afterwards.

"The opposite of you." He regretted saying anything. They knew each other well enough already. It is possible to know people too well. He patted her flank, that rich muscular thigh.

"What happened to her?"

Bian in her ivory and gold *ao dai*. Bian with bare feet in the mud. Bian naked in the mud, her body brown with it. It's raining. Middie has a bandanna around his neck and no shirt on. The person he most wants to take revenge on isn't a Vietcong. It's Pell. He has told Bian he will pay her big moneys if she removes her clothes and crawls on all fours through the mud.

"Like soldier do. Like soldier in jungo." He speaks his language mockingly, worse than Bian speaks. "Good soldier shoot naked in jungo."

A crowd is gathering. Pell isn't around; he's holding someone down in the medical tent, a young guy who came in with part of his jaw blown off. Pell hears about "jungo" later, about the absurd sum Middie said he would pay Bian.

"I don't think we should follow this line of conversation any further," Pell says. Some bedrock level in him feels unstable.

"But I want to know." Elizabeth props herself up on an elbow. "Tell me." She pinches his nostrils closed and holds them there like a safety pin. He bats her arm away.

He changes the story. Bian is back in her hut with chocolates and a paper lantern. She's sleeping peacefully with Middie's big American money in the folds of her dress. He saved her from Middie, from being serially raped by all of them, anyone who wanted to join in. He did save her. He did.

Now the hour of doom is upon them. He wraps a towel around his waist. She has no one to return to, no reason to shower off their smell. On the television the debate is about which qualifies as the world's tallest building. There is a tall buildings committee that will decide. She dozes in the room's dry heat.

He soaps his armpits, his ears that she licked and the scrotum to which she paid her delicate attentions. Lather away the mud. Make for memory a shroud and not a window. He soaps the bottoms of his old feet. One of them will betray him. *Who invented the human heart? Tell me, and then show me the place where he was hanged.*

He is recalling this line from his favorite novel when his foot catches on the lip of the tub. It is not his foot that has betrayed him but the vessels supplying blood to his brain.

"Oh God. Let me help you up." She is naked above him, her hair in a curtain over one shoulder. That dark pudenda.

"Get your things and go. Call 911 and go. Please."

"Please?"

She speaks on the phone with the concision of the lawyer she will be. Dresses quickly.

"I want to wait with you." Her hand on his forehead.

A blood clot that forms somewhere in the body and breaks off to become free-floating is an embolus.

"No. Please go, Elizabeth." An officer's command. She is agitating him. *He thought and suffered a good deal but he lacked the resolution to dare.* We will never know anyone's last thoughts.

He lies crumpled in the bathroom. She gathers the Party Box and condom wrappers. The empty wine bottle and cups. It is so important to rid the room of evidence. Both her hands are full. She does not think to take the key.

The Volvo is the only car in the lot. She has forgotten until this moment that she rode with him. She will wait near the dumpster and watch from across the lot as the ambulance pulls up. She has disposed of their afternoon as he asked. In the years to come she will tell close friends that she held his head in her lap as he died.

In the Wasp Kingdom

Kenny grabs one of the laminated sheets. Ann grabs the other laminated sheet. In front of them they both have XL Energy Cokes. For those two that is a lot of Energy Coke. Pat O'Shea walks by and swipes Kenny across the forehead. Sometimes it's like we're all back in high school and Pat O'Shea is the assistant principal. Probably Kenny should have moved to another part of the room when Ann sat down, or Ann should have sat down somewhere else. They get in each other's hair. It's not good for either of their recoveries. Watching them get in each other's hair is also detrimental to other people's recovery. Picture a wasp having it out with another wasp, but both of the wasps being chased by guys with wasp killing spray. Kenny's sponsor says he engages when he needs to disengage and vicey-versey.

Sewn on Ann's new cigarette case is the face of a person who looks a lot like Ann with a martini glass tilted to her mouth and a red circle with a diagonal slash through it. All the arts and crafts Ann creates have an anti-alcohol theme. She won't do the anti-smoking theme until she quits smoking.

Kenny has himself a good look. "What's missing there is her busta-mientos."

"Take your hand out of your pants, Kenny."

Kenny, in a general address to everyone in the room: "All's I was making's an observation."

"Go make another sand mandala, Ken."

In reality Kenny isn't making anything, unless it's French fries. He's the kind of person who wears a bow tie to be funny. The way he holds his arms a little away from his body reminds me of an action figure I once had with arms you could pull and stretch. We pulled too much one time and clear syrup oozed out so we threw him away. You can do that with dolls.

Other people are milling around and getting settled, paying no attention to Kenny. Which is his problem. Which is a lot of our problems. Also, Kenny and Ann used to be married. Most of what goes on between them is some kind of marital replay. Under her breath Ann's asking God for the wisdom to know the difference.

At one end of the room an altar with a neon sign flashes *But for the Grace of God*. At the other end is a bar (a bar!) with white tile on the front and the two A's spelled out in blue tile. Five or six guys stand behind it and hand out coffee and smoke. The regulars sit at the desks in the middle. Hugging the walls are the brown plaid saggy sofas where newcomers or people who want to nap go.

The leaders today are the twins, Ilke and Thor, who look like they've stepped off a lacrosse field or a Norse ship. They start out by talking about Step 6, *Being entirely ready to have God remove these defects of character*. Thor with his straight white teeth talks about his defects of character. Ilke with her milky blemishless skin talks about her defects of character.

There's a pause while the rest of us think about how much better life would be if we had straight white teeth and blemishless skin and played lacrosse or stepped off a Norse ship and had sisters and brothers like Ilke and Thor. But you don't want to go too far down that road or you're back on the vodka breakfast.

Pat O'Shea reads the rationale for anonymity, and all in attendance play with the lip of their Styrofoam cup or take a drag of their cigarette. I admire the ones like Kenny who exude a certain alienated boredom.

Someone will be reading aloud about "Came to believe that a Power greater than ourselves could restore us to sanity," and Pat O'Shea will be fiddling with his watch or Kenny will be shifting the ice around in his Coke or Ann will be flicking lint off her shirt and eyeing Pat O'Shea.

There's authority in just having the routine down. Ann says *I'm Ann, and I AM an alcoholic.*

Everyone says *Hi, Ann.*

Sometimes Ann says *I'm Ann, and boy am I ever an alcoholic!*

Sometimes she says *Ann here, raging alcoholique.*

You never thought you would meet a person who enjoys pointing out her own alcoholism so much. But Ann is a go-to person if you really want to get better. She's been doing this for eons. In her drinking days, Ann pushed stuffing in her bra to satisfy Kenny's desire for bustamientos and tried to offset her snoot by costuming her head in a tall platinum wig, strategies she believed would be of interest to the male of the species, though I'm not sure the *numero uno* male in question was Kenny. Once they had a fight that left bite marks on Kenny's wrists.

I am not sure how badly I want to get better. I wonder where Ann keeps that wig.

Ann mentions how at the beginning of the meeting Kenny here referred to her craftwork solely in terms of its missing bustamientos, causing her to want to rearrange his face, but seeing as how she's been ready for a while to have God remove all defects of character, she refrained from socking or otherwise engaging Kenny.

Other than the hand in the pants remark.

"Which you deserved," Ann says.

"Your allotted five minutes are so up," Kenny says.

Ann is someone, according to the Big Book, to be emulated. You should "Stick with the winners." Though I am not sure from a certain perspective I would call Ann a winner. Myself, I am betting on Ilke and Thor. I am betting on Pat O'Shea.

Tonight I'm not the only newish one here. There's a woman about my age with watery eyes, wearing a yellow terrycloth halter dress. You go to these meetings, and if you're in bad shape you look to see who's worse.

Terrycloth Dress is worse.

"On the way here I stopped and bought a bottle," she says. "I'm wondering if someone can come with me to my car after the meeting and pour it out."

All the old-timers pipe up, and the women glare at Kenny and Pat O'Shea, who because of being males will not be chosen as the Pourers Out.

"I've been sober a long time," says Kenny. "I'm such a sicko, though, I'm sitting here wondering if the bottle she bought is anything I'd like."

"I'd like anything she bought," says Pat O'Shea.

At the end of the meeting Thor and Ilke ask who needs a temporary sponsor and since I promised myself, my hand goes up. They ask who's willing to *be* a temporary sponsor and Ann's hand goes up, which I was hoping it wouldn't. But sometimes, according to the Big Book, inspiration comes from unlikely places, and maybe Ann is mine.

I haven't killed anyone drinking but according to some reports I've gotten close (the black dog that night wearing a reflective collar so small you could barely see it; pedestrians too close to the road). My niece Appleby and I went down an embankment that left her wearing a bucket of onion rings, and I've got only a partial account of what happened between leaving the onion ring place and arriving down the embankment. But I am not like some of these people, i.e. Kenny, i.e. Ann, i.e. Thor and Ilke, i.e. probably Pat O'Shea, who have done unforgivable things to themselves and/or others.

After the meeting I stand outside with Kenny and Pat O'Shea and Thor while Ann and Ilke go with Terrycloth Dress to her car. Terrycloth Dress puts her headlights on and Ann pours out the bottle. We look and groan. It's just like Ann not to pour the bottle out where no one can see it, which is more Ann dolloping jam on the back of a wasp so its wings stick together.

Ann hugs Terrycloth Dress and they exchange of slips of paper. Then Ann comes over and gives me a slip of paper.

"Call me if you need to talk."

"I'm not that much of a talker."

"I'm not that much of a listener." She takes my hand between her two hands that feel like the pincers they use at parks to pick up trash.

Rheumatoid arthritis is another one of her day-to-day challenges, she says, along with Kenny, who has her in court all the time over custody of their daughter Maude and their beagle Cutty Sark.

Overall she has me beat in the talking department. Also in the daily challenge department.

Finally Ann's pincers let go. "It works if you work it," she says.

Which is what they always say.

I walk home through the woods behind the library. I'm not scared of the dark or getting raped or bitten. I'm scared of going home to my empty apartment and having to sit and then lie down and try to sleep. Days are easy. I've always been a night drinker.

I sit on my balcony and scratch my bare heels in the Astroturf. I sit at the kitchen table and read sales circulars from Belk.

I sit.

I put in my earbuds and walk back and forth from the kitchen to the balcony listening to songs on my iPod.

Back to the balcony.

Back to the kitchen.

Eight minutes away is the ABC Package Store, where there are bottles of wine and bottles of wine and bottles of wine.

When I wake it's light and I can't get my earbuds untangled from various limbs and my face hurts from pressing against Astroturf and I'm thinking this thought: The difference between trying to quit drinking compared to going through the death of a loved one or an illness like a brain tumor is a lot of difference.

Here is something that ends up happening to me. Or, sorry, that I end up creating, as I am chief cook and bottle washer of my own life.

I'm walking down the hill to the Big Book meeting Friday afternoon. As I put one foot in front of the other, each time a foot goes down I say to myself inside my head *I am not drinking, I am not drinking.* I know there should be a more positive message, but all I am capable of at this juncture is *I am not drinking.* Going to a meeting on a Friday afternoon is about the last thing I feel like doing other than taking my eyes out with a pair of pliers. There's a field between the woods, library, and road that leads down to the building where our meetings are held. It should be a park, but there's just a filled-in swimming pool and some concrete risers and overgrown grass no one bothers to mow.

Someone's sitting in the overgrown grass with a baseball cap pulled low who looks to me as I get closer like Pat O'Shea.

He's looking down as he waves at me.

"You going over?"

"Come sit." He pats the overgrown grass next to him, then looks at his palm as if someone's punctured it. He has a blade of grass sticking out of his mouth.

I sit.

"You drank this week."

I didn't drink Thursday night. I sat and flipped through this week's Belk ad again (Why do we not boycott cable-knit sweater vests forever?) and listened to my iPod and washed the crust out of my Astroturf and walked from the balcony to the kitchen, balcony to kitchen, and got in bed and didn't drink.

"I'm talking about Wednesday."

"Wednesday?" Wednesday, when I drank a bottle and a bottle and maybe even an eensy part of another bottle, was seventeen centuries ago. I am so over Wednesday.

"You don't remember."

If you drink, three words you never want to hear put into a sentence together are those ones. Even "cauliflower ear incurable" is better. Even almost "death by hanging."

"The phone call?" Pat O'Shea says.

In the wasp kingdom, the female possesses an egg tube or ovipositor that doubles as a venomous stinger. The male can't sting.

"Round about 3:00 a.m.?"

O Belk, with your sad dependable cable-knit sweater vests. O earbuds that stifle ambient noise. O Astroturf, scrubbed of puke and smelling now of vanilla lavender disinfectant.

"And I came over?"

As someone feeds you pieces of it, the contours of the evening usually emerge out of the gloom. No contours emerge. All I remember is Belk-earbuds-balcony-wine-wine-wine.

"With Ann?"

"With ANN?"

Pat O'Shea nods his big head that I like because it's always easy to see his facial expression, except in this case, when he's wearing the baseball cap. "You really don't remember."

Me wanting to save face or wanting to postpone his story, I admit Wednesday was a Bad Day, and a Bad Day is an especially Good Reason to go to a meeting. I try to say it the way Thor and Ilke do, *exspecially.*

"Okay, well, let's just say maybe you want to apologize to Ann for the bites on her wrists."

Contours distinctly emerging.

Wednesday late, after the walk to the ABC Package Store and the walk back, during which I sipped some of my purchases from a cup I brought along for just that purpose, I apparently got it in my head to phone Appleby. Since the onion ring/embankment incident, my sister has been wary about letting Appleby spend unsupervised time with her aunt. I call Appleby on her cell, and we have a chat, and I offer to come pick her up, we could get more of those onion rings and maybe catch a movie. There are some things I'm vague about, but I'm not vague about the onion rings, and I distinctly remember being a little peeved when Appleby insisted that the onion ring place would already be closed. At which point, apparently, Appleby and I quarreled, and I called Pat O'Shea (according to Pat O'Shea) to ask if he knew what time the onion ring place closed.

One thing I left out is I called Pat O'Shea from my moving vehicle. Which, I admit, slipped my mind. My thinking was Get Appleby, get onion rings, eat onion rings with Appleby, catch movie. And if the onion ring place was in fact closed, Appleby and I could stop at a convenience store and get the closest thing to onion rings (maybe pork cracklins) and park down by the river and have a nice aunt-to-niece talk and eat them. Which would have been fine, except for the interference of Pat O'Shea and also Ann, whom Pat O'Shea called to meet me, where else, up the embankment, which is apparently where I landed. I must have a soft spot for embankments.

At some point it is alleged I asked Ann about that wig and Ann said she didn't have it or I couldn't have it and I possibly, according to Pat O'Shea, bit her.

There are two main categories of wasp, solitary and social. If you put jam on the females' wings, they will get angry and fly around and sting. Up to a thousand wasps live in a social colony, though only the queen and male wasps mate. The rest are sterile female workers.

Around Pat O'Shea and me the insects buzz and dive. I scratch three new welts. "Nobody got hurt, right? Other than Ann's wrists a little?"

"I'll tell you who got hurt," Pat O'Shea says.

In my head I say please don't say me. Maybe I am stupid and a little bit dehydrated, but I am not hurt.

"Me," says Pat O'Shea. "Your friend Pat O'Shea got hurt, because he had to see the woman he loves crawling around on all fours like a dog and biting Ann's wrists over something about a wig."

I'd been thinking maybe I was getting the We Had Sex vibe from Pat O'Shea. Now I see I was on the wrong track completely. The Woman He Loves vibe? I didn't even know that was a vibe. As I'm trying to see if any of the contours of Pat O'Shea and me Loving Each Other emerge from the gloom, what emerges from the woods is a woman in a bad wig and a T-shirt and jeans with red slashes and a bandage over her nose.

Appleby!

I always give Appleby a hug, which is one thing I can do in addition to onion rings to compensate for my sister naming her after a chain of mediocre restaurants just because that's where she met her husband.

"I've been walking," Appleby says. "Thinking about our time up the embankments." She's still holding my arm and hugging me and getting wet spots that are red on my shirt. "I've been walking all around town without stopping except for the occasional beverage and thinking how the sway of alcohol over mankind is unquestionably due to its power to stimulate the mystical faculties of human nature—"

To which I say it's certainly the case that "Sobriety diminishes, discriminates, and says no. While drunkenness expands, unites, and— pardon me, Mr. O'Shea—says yes." Wet spots be damned (Appleby just got snagged on a few branches wandering around in the woods), I bid farewell to Pat O'Shea and tell him have a good meeting and sorry about the tooth marks, Ann. Appleby wants me to go to the woods with her, and what I want to do is go to the woods with Appleby.

In the woods are birds and mosquitoes and berries and the small happiness of the rustling of animals' paws in leaves; also a cooler Appleby stashed with ice in it and beer. We sit on pine needles. We open beers.

One thing we're able to establish about Wednesday is we—me and Pat O'Shea—definitely didn't have sex.

"We had wine," Appleby says. "Then you drove your car and then I drove your car and then we had a Chinese fire drill and you drove again and then for a while we were up the embankment, where you taught me the words to 'American Pie' and we sang it and you told me what it was like to be alive when the Beatles were still together and losing your virginity with 'Fool on the Hill' playing on the stereo."

My niece has a very shining face, and I'm appreciating it when the contours emerge from Wednesday about the piece of information she told me, which was important, which I'd semi-forgotten, how she was thinking about losing her virginity with Mike Sandbold, which I said maybe she'd want to think about, not because I had anything against losing virginity but because other than Mike Sandbold's playing for the football team she couldn't come up with a list of things she liked about Mike Sandbold.

We're having our third or *maybe* fourth beer and enjoying the birds in the woods when a bigger rustle overcomes the small rustle of paws and around some trees comes Pat O'Shea, and then who else but Ann and Kenny.

"Not only are you drinking, but you're drinking with an underaged minor," Ann says. Kenny kneels next to me and leans in like he's trying to get the fumes off my beer, but really what he's doing is stroking my hair, which in a nonmystical state I wouldn't be sure about having Kenny do but after maybe four beers it seems like a gesture I should properly acknowledge, so I return the favor and stroke his.

So we are sitting there on the forest floor hair-stroking, my niece enjoying for one of her first times the internecine struggles of adults.

"The question is," I say. My train of thought's the runaway caboose of my intentions, so I start again. "The question is whether you want to be the wasp flying around and having its shining day or the person chasing it down into the basement with a can of wasp killer."

"Ordinarily I wouldn't climb up here, Miss Beer-in-the-Woods-with-an-Underaged-Minor," Ann says. "Ordinarily I would let you dig your own pit, especially when you're getting yourself going on a bender."

I say that's *Ms.* Beer in the Woods. I say I'm good at digging pits.

"You may remember from just a few days ago a woman in a yellow terrycloth dress."

I picture the dress, the watery eyes, the booze Ann poured out in the headlights. "That woman? Let's say because there are youngsters around that she has met her can of wasp killer. And let's say picture that can of wasp killer as a semitruck that our friend in the terrycloth dress had an unscheduled meeting with when her Ford Tempo hopped over on the wrong side of the median Thursday night."

Appleby burps and giggles.

The question I know I'm supposed to ask is about God removing all defects of character. It's about a Power greater than ourself restoring ourself to sanity. It's about ourself being powerless over alcohol. But the question ourself wants to ask is about joy. Sure I puke, sure I'm bleary in the a.m. and my liver is going lacy around the edges. But what about the uniting, expanding, and saying yes? What about the keyhole I crawl through where on the other side are onion rings and chats with Appleby up the embankments and beers in the woods with the rustling?

"You can do that without the sauce," Ann says.

"No! no! no!" I do a No dance in the leaves, and Appleby gets up and does a No-ish-to-Maybe dance in the leaves along with me. The squirrels and birds rustle and dance and we rustle and dance. I put leaves in my hair that Kenny was stroking, though now he's looking at me as if he doesn't want to have a whole lot more to do with my hair.

"You can do without the sauce!" the sauce says. A can of beer's telling me from its can-mouth that I can live my big yes life.

To which I say no! and no! and no! and then I'm down in the leaves rustling and kicking and then I guess sleeping.

When I wake, it's night and everyone's gone. A note from Appleby says she had to go to audition for *Godspell* and clean her room. My hands are shaking as I walk up the hills home.

I will go to the meetings.

I will ask God to remove all defects of character. I will drink the energy Cokes and allow my earbuds to conduct through their squishy man-made fibers music about sunshine and gladness. I will molt from the shell of my former self. Appleby will benefit greatly from the example of her newly defectless aunt.

Over at Belk the hives of sweater vests shiver on their hangers and advance, advance, advance.

The Fleischer/Giaccondo
Online Gift Registry

The Crate & Barrel online gift registry displays columns headed WANTS and HAS, so that the prospective buyer (family and friends of, in this case, Lorraine M. Fleischer and Richard Giaccondo, M.D.) can compare the items the bride wishes to receive with the number already purchased for her. The bride, for instance, WANTS eight Birgitta Goblets and at this time HAS four Birgitta Goblets. She WANTS one Caliente Salsa Bowl w/Spoon, and yet as of 11:53 p.m. on this balmy night in May, she HAS zero Caliente Salsa Bowls w/Spoon. However, one cannot claim that events aren't unfolding in concert with the bride's wishes, because according to the Crate & Barrel online gift registry, as of this moment, the future Mrs. Richard Giaccondo WANTS one Gourmet Butter Spreader and indeed HAS one Gourmet Butter Spreader. She WANTS one Gravy/Sauce Boat Nautical and lo and behold she HAS one Gravy/Sauce Boat Nautical. She WANTS twelve Gourmet Flatware Placesets, and by God all twelve Gourmet Flatware Placesets are hers. Things, as they say, are coming along.

The morning after this balmy night, Lorraine's only sister would fly to Buffalo and don a full-length fuchsia taffeta gown with dyed-to-match shoes for the Fleischer/Giaccondo wedding. While so attired, she would field questions from family and friends of Fleischers and Giaccondos about her (*a*) "career," a grand misnomer for composition classes she teaches as an adjunct instructor at the state university near her "home" (garden-level apartment with a termite "situation" and permanent leakage in bathroom ceiling from upstairs shower). "Supplementary income" is earned from employment as a "consultant" in the "natural living" department of the local franchise of the chain health-food store in town. She would also be expected to account for her (*b*) marital status, which, though unchanged in thirty-four years, remains an inexhaustible topic of conversation. But at this moment, at 11:54 p.m. on a balmy night in mid-May, she sat with a stack of unread Composition 101 essays on her kitchen table and, in a moment of procrastinatory weakness engendered by three glasses of starter wine from a jelly jar, scrolled through the Fleischer/Giaccondo online gift registry. It was then that she, instead of reading essays that explained *Why the death penalty really improves our society* and *Why legalizing marijuana would really improve our society,* came to observe the vast and orderly domestic tableau being constructed around the other Fleischer sister, one Buffet Cheese Plane Stainless ($26.95) at a time.

The maid of honor, though having consented to outfit herself in fuchsia taffeta and dyed-to-match shoes, was often referred to, with varying degrees of tolerance, as "bohemian." Evidence of said bohemianism could be found in the contents of the maid of honor's travel duffel, which included two drop-waist dresses made from hemp plants, a tube of natural toothpaste (anise flavor) manufactured without fluoride or artificial flavorings and dyes in the woods of Maine, a 100% cotton reusable sanitary napkin that provoked a stifled but nonetheless audible snort of disgust from the bride-to-be, and a small embroidered bag, handmade by a Guatemalan artisans cooperative, which contained a blue glass pipe adorned with a yin-yang symbol and a small plastic baggie, the contents of which, had the maid of honor not carefully concealed them, would have provoked from the bride-to-be an even more audible snort of disgust.

In the year since the announcement of the engagement, an unacknowledged but nonetheless palpable tension had developed between the bride and the maid of honor. Reasons for said tension include but are not limited to the following:

1. Unarticulated but seething-just-below-the-surface disagreement between bride and maid of honor about ethics of spending $40,000 on a wedding reception.

2. Maid of honor's pointed and frequent references to insurmountable burden of student load debt combined with status as adjunct instructor sans health insurance. Hence, maid of honor possesses teeth upon which root canals overdue, cervix for which pap smear overdue, etc. Loan, teeth, cervix repeatedly invoked while referring to cost of fuchsia gown and shoes.

3. Bride's deep-down suspicion that spending $40,000 on wedding reception might in fact be ethically indefensible.

4. Various unresolved sibling rivalries.

❧

At the rehearsal dinner, held at Lorenzo's Ristorante in a comfortable Buffalo suburb, the maid of honor was introduced for the first time to her ceremonial counterpart.

"I don't know about the superlatives," the best man said. "I could be the Best-Available-at-This-Time Man. I could be the Not-Bad-for-a-Man Man."

Which would mean the maid of honor could aspire to be the Maid of Middling Respectability. "Though I always said I'd never be a maid or have one," the maid of honor said.

"Better to have than to be, indeed." The best man frowned. "I sound like a bad Shakespeare imitator. Do you want a cocktail, a cigarette, crudité?"

And so it came to pass that, after watching a lengthy video production that patched together images of a combined fifty-two years in the lives of the bride and groom, and after boogeying to disco hits of the 80s in the enthused but vaguely apologetic manner in which people dance to songs they believed exemplars of musical genius a decade or two earlier but now acknowledge to be tacky and embarrassing remnants of a former age (the maid of honor blushed while leaping in time to the Go-Go's "Our Lips Are Sealed"; the best man couldn't make eye contact with the maid of honor during Duran Duran's "Hungry Like the Wolf"), the best man and the maid of honor came to a mutual (if unspoken) decision.

It was at this time that the bride and groom announced that they would return to their apartment to rest up for the following day's events. The best man, in a manner consonant with the duties of a best man, volunteered to ferry the maid of honor back to her sister's apartment at some later but as-yet-undesignated time. This decision was made in the haphazard way decisions get made when all participants in the decision-making process are scrambling to come to terms with that point in the evening's festivities when the bar's designation switches suddenly from OPEN to CASH.

It was, however, explained by the bride that although she could give the maid of honor a spare key to gain entrance to their building, the bride did not have an extra key to the apartment door with her. Therefore, the maid of honor would have to ring the bell when the best man brought her back. The maid of honor suggested that the bride and groom hide the spare key under the mat outside their door, to which the bride responded somewhat mincingly that *under the mat* did not constitute a *legitimate hiding place*, so if she was really going to *stay out gallivanting*, they would have to *ring her in*.

To which she (I) conceded.

It was clear, if not to everyone at least to the maid of honor, that the overwrought negotiations about entrances and keys and hiding places and gallivanting had everything to do with the aforementioned palpable tension and nothing whatsoever to do with entrances, keys, etc.

I saw it. I saw that the bride didn't want the maid of honor gallivanting. I saw that the bohemian adjunct maid of honor was not to gallivant or otherwise fraternize inappropriately with any member of the Giaccondo clan.

But she was my *little* sister, and I was a *thirty-four-year-old* woman, and we were in a room full of *future in-laws,* and there was already enough palpable tension between the two of us to light an internal combustion engine, and on top of all that it was plain to see (even I could see) that, by some delightful inconsistency in the workings of the universe, and in spite of the shapeless hemp dress and a face unenhanced by so much as a drop of concealer or eyeliner or blush, the best man, a respectable wage earner and homeowner and a Giaccondo through and through, had the hots for the bride's sister.

Had the hots for *me.*

And I, prospective owner of neither Gourmet Butter Spreader nor Caliente Salsa Bowl w/Spoon; I, whose plates have never matched *each other,* I, who for the most part am content to drink starter wine from a jelly jar; I, bohemian adjunct badly in need of a pap smear and two root canals, was enjoying it.

It was not long after the departure of the bride and groom that the maid of honor and the best man said their good-byes and buckled themselves into his Volkswagen Passat. Neither made any reference whatsoever to their destination. They drove along for several minutes in awkward anticipatory silence.

"I have to make a decision here," the best man said at an intersection. "About what?"

"About whether we're going to my place or your sister's. They're in different directions."

The maid of honor's ceremonial counterpart had been stuck wrestling with the delicate issue of how, quite literally, to navigate the territory before him. It was dicey driving when you've consumed three or perhaps four vodka tonics, not a lot by the driver's estimation but enough to arouse the interest of the law if the law was, as it frequently is on a Saturday night, out patrolling for recreational drink-and-drivers. It was also dicey to have in the passenger seat of your Passat the sister of the woman your first and favorite cousin is going to marry, particularly when she's (A) lit and (B) could at this point without a whole lot of prodding be persuaded to come back to your house.

"I should probably go home," said the maid of honor. "They'll worry about me."

"No problema, señorita." The best man was in this instance really going to try to be the best man and not get tangled up in the ethical boondoggle of sweet-talking into bed a soon-to-be relative by marriage. Though he would be hard-pressed to come up with the term that designates the familial relationship between the sister of the bride and the first cousin of the groom. It would one thing if the sister of the bride stated clearly and unequivocally or even not so clearly and unequivocally that she wouldn't mind going back to his house with him well after midnight on a Saturday and another entirely if he took it upon himself to deliver this woman, with neither a car nor her bearings nor at this point if he was honest with himself most of her powers of judgment, to his house.

He would ferry her back to the bride's.

But it is she—let the official transcript show—who suggests just blocks from the bride and groom's apartment that they detour into the parking lot of the Albright-Knox Gallery.

"Just for a little bit. We could sit and talk."

In the lot, the best man cuts the engine. They sit in silence and listen to the ticking of the car engine cooling. There is no one else around.

He unbuckles his seatbelt and swivels to face her. "You had fun at the rehearsal dinner?"

"I did," she says. "Now that I know you and your family a little, I'm going to have more fun at this wedding than I thought—I mean, it's not exactly a picnic when you're thirty-four and single and have to shoehorn yourself (*impossible-to-resist exaggeration as form of self-pity*) into a hot-pink gown for your younger sister's wedding, especially when you don't even know if you *believe* in weddings; I mean if you don't know if you can get behind the *symbolism* of the white dress and the veil, much less what all of it represents, which is of course the nuclear family," she's telling him, and she's really getting cranking on her objections to the commodification of marriage as evidenced by the colossal wedding industry and the Crate & Barrel online gift registry, also her objections to taffeta gowns and dyed-to-match shoes (*Jesus do they have to be fucking fuchsia?*), and if she's going to be completely honest her shock and offense at the fact that her sister plans to take the Giaccondo name, when the best man leans over and, in fulfillment of the unspoken contract they have been drawing up all evening, kisses her.

She's kissing him back, and his tongue is wandering sweetly in her mouth, and there's a moment when the thought occurs to her, as it always does when the tongues are wandering sweetly—she wouldn't want to admit it but there it is and it is this: *I could marry this one.* She hasn't thought this of every man she's kissed in the past five years, only the ones worth remembering: a macrobiotic chef who fed her edible flowers he grew in his backyard, a classical composer who called and played Gershwin and Rachmaninov on her answering machine, an ex-composition student who taught her the word *brindle* and how to dip menthol Skoal, a writer twenty years older who emailed daily love notes like exquisite novels in miniature but in the end said he was too old for her he had divorce kids he had moss growing on his antlers it would never work he was too old.

They will pause in their affections. They will wipe their mouths with the backs of their hands.

This might be a very good time to reach into her Guatemalan bag and take out the blue glass pipe adorned with the yin-yang symbol. They will pass the pipe back and forth and sit looking out the windshield at the Albright-Knox Gallery, which at this moment houses twenty-seven of Monet's lesser-known paintings. It is a building built for the purpose of housing art. A house where paintings live. She knows she must be feeling the effects a little when she hears herself think this and then say, *Damn, art is great;* she wishes she were a painter or a composer; even a writer would be okay instead of teaching composition part-time at the state university and working in the natural living whatever-the-fuck-that-is-these-days department of the chain health-food store.

"That's something impressive, though—teaching college students," the best man says, moving toward her again. The maid of honor is drunk and stoned, but that doesn't mean she can't hear the way he's answering her perfunctorily so they can get past the talking, which she's all of a sudden interested in doing, and into the heavy petting, as if they're sixteen-year-olds on a first date rather than full-fledged adults acting out what amounts to an embarrassing homage to adolescence. If one of them puked right now, that would be the capper. But no one is puking. He's kissing her neck and then she's kissing his neck and while the two of them are struggling within the admittedly narrow parameters of the bucket seats of the Passat to demonstrate with wandering tongues how impassioned each of them makes the other, her mind wanders to a night-class Composition 101 she was teaching the semester her sister announced her engagement. It was the last class, and students were reading their essays aloud, and one, the only black kid in class, volunteered to read his essay about *some important aspect of your identity*, and he stood up and read, *I am a singer, with my two brothers.* She had expected him to write about being black and oppressed or black and not oppressed or in any case black, and when instead it was *I am a singer,* tears surprised her and the class came to a standstill, including the kid reading his essay, while she blew her nose and tried to get her shit together, everyone asking what was wrong since it wasn't even one of the sad essays like the one by the woman who trained seeing-eye dogs and had to give each one up just when her kids couldn't help themselves anymore and fell in love with it, though that essay made her cry too, not so much for the dogs and kids but for the predicament every semester, the students coming in not especially liking her and not wanting to be in Composition 101, all of them knowing if they hadn't screwed up the placement exam they wouldn't have to take this class in the first place, and then writing and talking and writing and talking until she liked them and they liked her and just at the moment they were all ready to enjoy each other, the semester was over and they were gone.

The best man's hand had during this reverie crept beneath her drop-waist hemp dress. "Come here," he said. *Here* meant over the gearshift and onto his lap, but climbing over the gearshift would eventually lead to a logistical problem involving a 100% cotton reusable sanitary napkin; and even if by some miracle she managed to finesse that hygienic hurdle, she didn't relish the idea of her younger sister in a white gown and veil walking down the aisle of a church while she, the *Maid of Honor* after all, decked out in fuchsia dress, fuchsia shoes, a walking scarlet letter, witnessed the consecrated event of marriage knowing she had the previous evening in the front seat of a Passat in the parking lot of an art gallery housing twenty-seven of Monet's lesser-known paintings climbed over the gearshift and in a hemp dress and reusable sanitary napkin unceremoniously fucked the best man.

The best man and maid of honor kept holding on to each other then. His hand stayed under her hemp dress, but without the caressing and stroking it was like a small animal that had gotten in where it didn't belong, and it was a relief to both of them when he retrieved it and put it back on the steering wheel.

He turned the key. The radio came on. America was playing "Tin Man."

—in the back of the volare with patchwork sleeping bags matching fake patchwork driving down 95 over the bridge home from connecticut christmas day & them in the front seat singing tin man and her saying one of my favorite songs but he shouldntve written it that way with two didnts right in a row & just like that the whole day clattering down around them how she hated it at his mothers the drinking the hymns and angels the fake religion and him saying oh geez don't ruin it now denise & us squinched up next to each other in back in matching sleeping bags trading back and forth the colors of skittles we liked we liked different colors of skittles & always traded—

The best man opened the glove compartment. From it he retrieved a roll of breath mints. He ran a finger under her eye that was closest to him.

"Are you crying?"

The tears running down her face confirmed that she was indeed crying, but she hastened to assure him that it was nothing, just the song that was playing. She considered telling him about her and her sister, little girls in the back of the Volare, and their long since-divorced parents singing along to the eight-track stereo and as the years went on singing less and quarreling or silent more. But in the next instant she decided the best man wasn't the sort to grapple with the sentimental outpourings of women. He was, after all, by his own admission a Best-Available-at-This-Time Man. A Not-Bad-for-a-Man Man. Which was not to say he wasn't a nice person, running his finger under her eye and noticing the tears. It was just that he was also the person who sang into the air microphone of his hand when Sinatra's "Summer Wind" (designated Our Song by the bride and groom) began playing after the Duran Duran song ended. She had been hoping he would slow-dance with her, as the bride and groom were, but he had opted for the schlocky bit with the air microphone instead.

The Passat's console clock read 3:27 when the best man delivered the maid of honor to the bride and groom's apartment building.

"See you at the altar," he said.

And then, to stave off the inevitable moment when the bell to 6N would have to be rung and its inhabitants awakened from their prenuptial slumbers, the maid of honor, instead of taking the elevator, opted to climb five flights to the apartment, during which time she contemplated the strange scrambling of destiny's order that stood the younger daughter at the threshold of marriage and all the respectable trappings of adulthood that such unions entail (e.g. mortgage, progeny, life insurance, Caliente Salsa Bowl w/Spoon), while the elder daughter went on in her aimless way with rendezvous in parking lots and starter wine in jelly jars.

Several things happened after the maid of honor knocked on the door of 6N. For the sake of brevity, I will summarize. A small late-night scene, the subject of which: gallivanting. Then the fold-out sofa. Then a few hours of turbulent sleep.

The next was the wedding day. All typical and blurry. Morning frantic frantic frantic. Bride wants. Bride has. Wants wants wants. No no no. All wrong. Raining. Drizzling. Drizzle. Rain. Umbrellas, procure umbrellas. Raining raining fuchsia.

Procession. Do you take this. Do you take this. Lawful lawful. Loveonhercherish. Drumroll. Kiss. (Maid of honor glances, best man winks). Procession. Throw rose petals not rice. Open bar open bar open bar. Air microphone electric slide macarena bunny hop. Buffet buffet ice sculpture steak or salmon. Bouquet throw. Bouquet throw no catch. Click click heels adios fuchsia. Sleep bye home fly delay airport delay pull mask over face breathe normally bag may not inflate in case of emergency.

In case of an emergency, the flight attendant announced, *your seat cushion can be used as a flotation device.*

We have these rituals. They are what we have.

Okay, we passengers agreed to say. *Okay.*

Love in Wartime

I

On the north side of Dublin, across the street from a big church beside a pub called The Confession Box, Sarah watches a group of smokers get used to the new law in the rain. This neighborhood has a down-at-the-heels look that seems almost willful, as if no one really wanted the fanfare of all these columns and pilasters just for religion. Though actually (consulting her guidebook), St. Mary's Pro-Cathedral, built in 1816, was meant to be hidden on a side street "to avoid inciting anti-Catholic feeling." If it had been built on O'Connell Street, the English might have torched it.

At the foot of the church steps, a woman pulls something out of a trash bin and shoves it in a pillowcase. Her clothes and hair look as if they've been tended to fairly recently, but when Sarah asks whether Dublin has a special city code to use when dialing from a cell phone, the woman opens and closes her mouth without making any sound, then shakes her head and looks away. She has discolored teeth the color of tea and worn to nubs. The rain doesn't seem to affect her.

The rain has done Sarah a favor: The anorak she borrowed for this trip is a men's medium, much too large for her, all-concealing. She has stuffed her documents and money in the zippered front pocket. Her kangaroo pouch.

A vigorous older man with a quiff of gray hair hurries muttering down Marlborough Street. Sarah hears what she thinks is a snatch of a psalm. Seeing the suitcase, he pulls up in front of her and pumps her hand. "Jerry Farrell. I'm late, apologies, apologies. Míle Fáilte!" He ushers her along and lets her inside the tall black metal gate.

"This is a secure place you've chosen. You'll have no trouble here."

Most of the apartment buildings look to be from the late '6os and early '7os, that utilitarian era for public housing.

"Sarah," Jerry Farrell says. "That's a biblical name."

Now that they're inside the gates, a stalk of strength in her revives, like a droopy plant that has taken in water. The building where Jerry leads her is a low, pinkish gray box, a far cry from the Georgian architecture in better Dublin neighborhoods, but she has reason to hope it'll at least be quiet and somewhat clean.

"Oh, wait, I've a sheet with the codes you need to get in and out." He heads back to a beat-up car. She follows and tries to read a sandwich board in the trunk with slogans on it. Something about the end times.

"Hope the rain lets up. I've an appointment with the Lord in Mountjoy Square!"

Just like that, as if he and the Lord meet every Thursday for coffee.

"What they do now," he says as he punches a code that lets them into the building, "what they do is come here just before they're due, to have the baby on Irish soil."

"Who does?"

"The Nigerians." He's looking at some forms she must have filled out online. "Will your husband be joining you?"

"He's flying in tomorrow." The words come out evenly; she doesn't garble them with stuttering or blushing.

"So the two of yourselves. Very good. The Nigerians, as I was saying, five or six of them will be here at any one time. The whole lot of them nine months along. I won't let to them anymore; they take a place to pieces."

The flat is a low-ceilinged warren of rooms crowded with forced signs of cheerfulness: potted red plastic flowers, a large Lucite disc hanging in the kitchen window with a faux needlepoint sampler inside that reads *Jesus Loves Me,* stuffed bears wearing T-shirts that say "Hug Me," "Love Makes the World Go 'Round, a pagoda mobile that looks like something nicked from a Chinese restaurant.

The first thing she'll do is put them in a closet.

After Jerry waves good-bye, she tries to close the blinds and they come crashing down. For sure Jerry would blame the Nigerians. She pulls a chair in from the kitchen and stands on it to work at putting them up again, until she's dizzy from the effort. The blinds will have to wait. She turns on the TV and lies down on the creaky sofa where a few weeks ago the Nigerians must have rested. On television, the British prime minister is fielding questions from an interviewer about the invasions in the Middle East. The *mea culpa* implied in the way he reacts to the questions, even in the way he sits and listens and sniffs, as if able to smell the artillery fire for which he's partly responsible—all of it is so much easier to watch than the American president with his malapropisms and his chin thrust forward. In a few minutes she's asleep.

❧

On a night in September two years ago, Sarah sat on the front porch of Phyllis O'Shea's house, a century-old bungalow painted vermilion. The sun had set, but temperatures in Alabama still hovered in the eighties. All the ceiling fan did was move the hot air around. The two of them had drunk the decent Pinot Grigio Sarah brought and then the rotgut Phyllis kept for nights like this. The folk-art gourds hanging by wires from the rafters had begun to look to Sarah like big misshapen ears. She went and got two glasses of soda water from the kitchen. Phyllis regarded hers with one eye closed, then got up and poured it vengefully into the cat's dish.

Phyllis's eyes drifted closed, but she snapped them open in a comedic, Gracie Allen way and went on as if she hadn't been close to passing out at all. "In my class there's one, too, *a brilliantly articulate young fellow named Derek,*" she said, lampooning Sarah wasn't quite sure what. "I would like very much to give him the pleasure of my company. Or, to be more specific, open my legs for him."

"It's not just about wanting to have sex," Sarah said. "He's this smart, sensitive guy. We have great conversations."

"Go have conversations, then. Just don't have relations."

You could never have a discussion with Phyllis about men without her acting as if it was her job to uncover your vulgar intentions. She treated you as if all you had was a giant raging id, and her job was to be your superego and slice you down to a narrow stalk of goodness. Which, given the size of Phyllis's id, was a pretty ironic proposition.

"What I'm saying is, I don't just want to sleep with him."

"You want a *relationship*." Phyllis blinked slowly, and Sarah thought she might conk out sitting up. Then Sarah would have to get her inside and help take her clothes off. Phyllis was nearly fifty, twenty years older than Sarah, which was why sometimes Phyllis treated Sarah like a friend and sometimes like a daughter. Plenty of times Sarah had helped unhook the clasps on one of Phyllis's big, complicated bras—devices Phyllis claimed she bought at the same shop in England where the Queen brought hers. The bras looked like prosthetic torpedoes. What did men do with all that flesh? Once, when Sarah and Phyllis went shopping, they stepped out of their fitting rooms at Ann Taylor and both were wearing the same dress, sand-colored with small white polka dots, a high neck, and a pin-tucked waist.

"Darling, you look like an emery board," Phyllis said. She was right. The dress was meant for Phyllis, petite and shaped like a small but substantial hourglass. Phyllis was originally from Dublin, but she had lived in the States since graduate school and had been teaching in Alabama for fifteen years. She had a let's-all-throw-ourselves-down-on-the-floor -since-that-will-surely-accomplish-something view of life.

Phyllis's one mantra, hammered in like a nail to a plank all the time but especially when she was drunk, was that a woman should own property and have children on her own if she wanted to. She divined a house in Sarah's future. Sarah saw a corps of broad-shouldered women holding property titles tied in scrolls with red ribbon.

"You don't mean a man for property or kids," Phyllis said.

"Don't *need* a man," Sarah said.

Phyllis went on without seeming to hear the correction.

"Oh, how you bore me. I'm ringing off!"

Was this an indirect hint that she should leave? Two of her colleagues, a lesbian couple who seemed uninterested in gossip or high drama, had warned her that Phyllis could get a little maudlin when she drank. But none of this felt maudlin. Instead, this was the bright, unexpected heat of female friendship, returning to her after the long exile of her twenties. Those years had been for anorexia and men. At one point in college she had gotten so thin she had grown a secret pelt on her stomach. Later she learned it had a name that she then went around chanting in her head. *Lanugo lanugo lanugo.* Out of the gray forest of skinny legs that had been her twenties she saw the solid peach flesh of herself come walking.

Phyllis had the old cat in her lap and was holding the dish of soda water.

"She won't like the fizzies," Sarah said. She lifted the dish out of Phyllis's hands and drank it.

"Fool!" Phyllis was coughing a laugh.

"Let's be everlasting," Sarah said. The word had a shine; it splashed over a brim she saw was happiness. Her happiness!

"Okay, Miss Happiness." The words came out slurred and a little nasty. Phyllis had had enough of her for one night. Sarah got up and waited to see if Phyllis would. When she didn't, Sarah took her hands and pulled her to her feet.

"Let's go feed your pets," she said.

"The pets," Phyllis said tenderly. She always fed her two cats right before bed. When she was drunk, she forgot. Then in the morning she felt terrible for forgetting. Mention of feeding them usually got her indoors, where she would clatter around the kitchen, moving dirty plates and glasses from one counter to another, then agree to go to bed.

In the dark bedroom, Sarah helped Phyllis undo her buttons and clasps. "Goodnight, Phyl," she said. She heard Phyllis grunt and give the pillow a few punches.

"I found one of those bugs in my pillow," Phyllis said.

"But not tonight," Sarah reassured her. Sometimes Phyllis seemed to hallucinate when she drank a lot.

"Stay away from them," Phyllis said.

That was what Sarah thought she said. Later, she realized she had misheard. *Stay away from him.*

Walking home, she thought about two gifts her mother had bought her for no occasion when Sarah was a teenager (on birthdays she had always gotten new clothes). Maybe the discussion about women buying property had triggered it. There was a card game called simply Women's Card Game, with grainy black-and-white photos of Julia Ward Howe, Sarah Orne Jewett, and Sojourner Truth on them. Sojourner Truth had a head like the blade of an axe. Also, the soundtrack recording for an off-Broadway show her mother had taken her to see. What was the name of it?

In the middle of the night she woke up massively dehydrated, mascara under her eyes. She would have to move very slowly and wing it with her classes the next day. The name of the show came to her: *I'm Getting My Act Together and Taking It on the Road.* She said it out loud. The early hours of the morning, Tuesday, September 11. She smiled in the mirror at her smeared, over-thirty face.

II

This part of the story everyone knows.

In class they are, they really are, studying Auden's "Musée des Beaux Arts." Sarah has lugged along a book with the Brueghel painting in it, because the students don't know what the hell he's talking about when he says "the dogs go on with their doggy life and the torturer's horse / Scratches its innocent behind on a tree." They think that's funny. Maybe it is funny.

Before class, she walked over to the Student Union to catch the news on TV. There'd been a special report on the public radio station she was listening to in her office. Already by then, TV stations were broadcasting images of a plane crashing into one of the Twin Towers. She watched the same footage three times and then went to teach.

In the middle of class she said, "I rather suspect that this day will turn out to be more historic than we at this particular moment can imagine."

They stared at her. If one of them had said it was a non sequitur, she might have felt improved. Most of them, young Alabama kids, didn't know what she was talking about. She never said things like "I rather suspect" or "this particular moment."

She let them out early. They were a sturdy group—that was how she would have described them. A couple of the guys held up a hand for her to slap as they left the room. She must have looked beleaguered for them to do that. Maybe their physical—or perhaps what she meant was physiological—health would protect them during the time ahead. She had an ominous longing to go back to the restricted, all-absorbing diets of her college years. It was the only way she knew of to manage the panic she felt coming on. Back to mashed bananas in the morning, cans and cans of Diet Coke, single-serving containers of Progresso lentil soup for dinner.

"Dr. Foy? Are you okay?"

He had waited for everyone else to leave the room.

"Just a little shaky, with all this."

"Is your family okay?"

He remembered her family was from New York. She had only made one small reference to that, when she mentioned they'd be reading *The Great Gatsby*. She'd said something she later wished she hadn't about how the novel was set in her neck of the woods.

"I could accompany you to your car," he said.

Ron Ajoloko had a wide mouth that she read as generous. Generous with what? He didn't maintain the neutral expression so many of her male students favored. That mouth was quick to smile or frown or drop open in surprise or question, and he had unusually square teeth with a space between the top two in front that was wide enough to be a feature in and of itself. He wore an oxford-cloth shirt and khakis, and he carried two thick books easily at his hip. She had thought about his hands opening a book to read a poem for her class or touching her face. One of his fingers running across the ridges of her bottom teeth.

"C'mon," he said, "let's get you out of here." He gestured with his head in the direction of the door.

"Your family?" Ron said again when they were out in the hallway.

"No one was near the Towers." Every time she allowed herself to think about what had happened, panic would rush in and make her gasp. To make it go away she'd have to think about getting skinny. *Lanugo. Lanugo.*

On their way downstairs, Ron pointed out that Cassandra was having a tough time getting comfortable in those desks. Cassandra was the
only very overweight person in the class. The classroom was equipped
with chairs with metal arms that reached around on the side and wid-
ened into a desktop. Sliding into the space between the chair back and
the desktop wasn't a problem for people of average size, but Cassandra
was top-heavy and had to perch at the edge of her seat. Worse, when
she arrived late (as she often did), the only desks left were an ancient
version of this style made of wood and carved many times over with
Greek letters and profanity. These had probably been built back in the
Eisenhower era, when people seemed to have been a lot smaller. Maybe
they could get a few plain old chairs for people to sit on and hold their
notebooks in front of them, Ron said. Or, since the class sat in a circle,
Cassandra could pull her chair up to the spot next to Sarah's desk and
lean her notebook on the edge of it. This would be an unobtrusive way
to deal with the problem until Sarah could inquire about getting new
classroom furniture.

"How strange that I missed that," she said.

No big deal, he said. His mother and aunt were big women, so he
tended to notice those kinds of things.

It was not true that Sarah hadn't noticed. The truth was that she felt
uncomfortable having Cassandra in her class. Was it that she was fat?
Smart? Black? Cassandra had such a soft voice that Sarah often had to
ask her to repeat herself. An exasperated look would cross Cassandra's
face, as if Sarah were hard of hearing. Sarah had ignored Cassandra's dis-
comfort in the desks, thinking that Cassandra's uneasiness would level
the playing field.

What playing field?

Her car was parked in the covered garage that was farther away;
there hadn't been any spots near her building.

"You don't need to walk me all the way up," she said.

Ron didn't say anything in reply, just kept along beside her. They
climbed the flights of cement steps up to the third level. She had
bought herself a Honda Civic recently, her first new-car purchase ever,
and her father had advised her to park it away from other cars if she

could, to prevent it from getting hit. There were only two other cars on this level.

"I could drive you home," he said.

"Then how would you get home?"

"You're close to campus, right? I can walk back."

She had mentioned that in class, too.

He had to hitch the driver's seat back as far as it would go. His size made the car seem small and insubstantial, like a toy.

"Which way?" he said, when they got to the intersection at University Boulevard.

"Any way," she said.

He seemed to take this directive as easily as if she were asking him to choose a poem to read out of *The Norton Anthology*.

"Do you mind if I turn on the radio?" he asked.

Her radio was set to NPR. "Is no trains runnin', is no buses runnin'," a man was telling a reporter. Sarah winced at the grammar and wondered if Ron did. Thankfully, the interview was short. Then a female reporter Sarah liked came on and said, "There's a keen sense of uncertainty about what lies ahead." After that, a bridge of classical music. It went on for so long that Sarah began to think the broadcasters had put the radio station on remote and evacuated, or that it had been vaporized by a bomb. Already it was possible to think these thoughts. Just hours ago she had been thinking about nothing much at all, gifts her mother got her when she was young and having to teach with a hangover.

"Can I turn it off?"

"Be my guest," he said.

A few miles and they were out of the city proper on a winding two-lane she would have derisively called a country road if she were describing it to her family. Areas so overgrown with kudzu vines that stop signs and telephone poles were engulfed alternated with dusty lots that contained a defunct shop and piles of tires or car parts or, in one instance, what looked to be rags and animal bones. Sometimes there were shacks with people sitting in porch rockers. Everyone Sarah saw was black.

"You know that part when he says, 'Children who did not specially want it to happen'? I was wondering why they didn't want it to happen."

It took her a second to figure out what he was talking about. "The Auden," she said.

"Yes."

She laughed and shook her head. The obstinacy of her mind was such that she didn't think she'd be able to come up with much to say about her favorite poem. She had done a dismal job in class.

"What do you think?" Her old pedagogical standby.

They went under a train trestle, and he pulled the car in behind one of the supports. Back here it was shady with the summer's overgrowth of bushes and kudzu. He turned off the engine. "I always think of Christ being the miraculous birth."

"Are you religious?"

"Some."

What did it mean to be "some"? Was it weedy and untended like her girlhood Catholicism?

Ron Ajoloko took her face in his hands. He kissed her on each ear first, then down and up her neck. She could picture the jagged cut he would have made if he had been after her with a broken bottle instead of his mouth. Sweat slid off his forehead onto her face.

When she got home there were six messages on her machine from Phyllis. They were pugilistic, paranoid, and finally resigned. In a death's-mask voice: "I am playing 'Adagio for Strings.'" There it was in the background, the soundtrack for waiting to see what life was going to be like next.

❧

"We're so fucked," said the man sitting next to her at Hale's Tavern. He was smiling. Some people liked this pain. It meant you didn't have to hear the bellyaching about healthcare or slavery reparations anymore. Now it was wall-to-wall terrorism. These attacks had come into being to test people's mettle, to show Americans what they were made of. Sarah was convinced she was made of something insubstantial and not renewable. After her grandmother's death, her mother had given her a lace table runner that fell into pieces when she went to lay it out. She felt like that.

The man patted her companionably on the back and offered her beer from his pitcher. "Don't you worry, the U.S. government will take care of you."

Tom Sloan was the sort of person who imagined himself made of something durable, like Astroturf. People called him Sloaney. His hair was cut in a style she had only seen on men in the South, full bangs grown down as far as the eyebrows and swept to one side. Later one of her colleagues would point to an undergraduate and refer to it as the Alabama Swoop. There was a gesture that went along with the haircut, a repeated toss of the head to get the hair out of the eyes.

He was a man about her age in jeans and a T-shirt with a grimacing elephant on the front. He said the news was bad, but Pearl Harbor was bad, too, and look how well we had come back from that. One of his eyes had a twitch.

"We'll get through this," he said. It was the sort of thing her father had said when the neighbor's boy threw a clump of burrs that got caught in her long hair. She'd made the mistake of trying to dislodge the burrs on her own, but she was panicked and had just tangled them more deeply. There had been a long afternoon on a picnic bench in her back-yard, her father working on her hair with scissors and a comb. In the end they had gotten through it, her father cutting away clumps of hair underneath. He had left the length intact, and she had calmed down, and he had been able to refrain from killing the boy, he said over the cheese-and-tomato sandwiches Sarah's mother brought out back, with a bottle of beer for her father.

Oh, yes, Tom said, he knew just the run-down Victorian on Queen City that Sarah described. He had known the former tenants, and he went to church with the guy who owned it.

On Saturday he came by. He was the type of person who comes by. "Nice what you've done with the place," he said. Which was nothing. She was just renting the bottom right half of a Victorian the owner seemed to be letting rot as an archaeological experiment. Tom said why didn't they go to Cabiness Paint and choose a color for the bathroom? The idea calmed her. She always got more interested in colors and music when she hadn't been eating.

So you could still go to the paint store and hold up color swatches against the wall and debate, as if people had not jumped to their deaths from a hundred stories up in a skyscraper. There was still that satisfying display of palettes from each designer with the colors starting at white and darkening slowly through the spectrum of pastels and then bright colors and then at the far end black. There was the pleasing noise like a bullet being shaken in a tin can that was the paint-mixing machine. The spatulate wooden sticks like giant tongue depressors for stirring the newly mixed paint. She noted each enjoyable thing, its tenor and degree. Everyone strove to be calm and polite; these were manners for a new era.

He took her west of town to a place he called Nick's in the Sticks. She pictured how the sign would look and what sort of sticks they would be and was disappointed when the building was just red with NICK'S written on it in white. Tom exchanged a man's hug with the guy running the show, a bearded black man wearing a T-shirt that said *You Don't Know Jack.* "Two Nicodemuses and a plate of gizzards," Tom said. Bright-red punch in Styrofoam cups with thick wedges of orange were placed in front of them. Was such a placid luxury allowed to exist? The ice cubes had grooves through the center of them. She piled them in her mouth, thinking how nice it would be if she were still a child and all she had to think about was the feeling of ice in her mouth. Then she remembered something. What was the deal with the sign on the way to the restaurant that said "Kozy Kristian Kottages?"

"What?" He was looking off in another direction. "I don't know. Nothing."

Sometimes, now, it was too tiring to argue. She had noticed that particular hue of fatigue setting in.

"I like the ice," she said.

"Well, good."

Tom was like that: "Well, good." He procured things for her: a used washer/dryer unit that he hooked up, hand-dipped chocolate pecans from a farmer he knew, a reliable exterminator. She worried about him meeting Phyllis without knowing why exactly she was worrying. Maybe because Phyllis would see he was a placeholder.

In class they were reading *Gatsby*. What a different world New York had been then, with quarrels in hotel lobbies and people drinking gin in the afternoon and renting rooms to sleep it off.

"Fitzgerald keeps saying people are doing or saying things 'with effort,'" Ron said. If anything he was more diligent and focused now in class. She saw she had been expecting him to swagger or not show up.

"They do?" she asked. She hadn't noticed and didn't believe him until he showed proof. She was only half-listening. Ron's question came to rest in airless silence. She scanned the class and tried to see their eyes without catching anyone's gaze. Did they know? Maybe he had told them. It was a ploy, a dare. The weather was still warm, and someone had opened a window. It let in the air from outside but also the drone of construction. All construction now made her think of Ground Zero, with its gray coating of ash on the heavy machinery. Machines had become ominous. They excavated the dead. She didn't like to drive. Crowds made her nervous. On a busy day in the Student Union she used the new bathrooms and thought maybe the toilet was wired to an explosive and would blow up when flushed. She hadn't told anyone about this line of thinking.

Ron paged through his copy of the book, then paused and looked bravely up at her. She could see he hadn't told anyone; he was in it right along with her. "I guess it just means they're having trouble going on."

He put his book face-up on the desk and pressed the spine flat. She could see his marginal notes and whole paragraphs underlined.

After class, he came by her office and sat while she gathered her books and shut down her computer.

"My favorite section's the one about the ash heaps." He paged hungrily through his book, found the passage, and began to read aloud. "This is a valley of ashes—a fantastic farm where ashes grow like wheat into ridges and hills and grotesque gardens; where ashes take the forms of houses and chimneys and rising smoke and, finally, with a transcendent effort, of men who move dimly and already crumbling through the powdery air."

It was her favorite part of the book, other than a section describing Gatsby's parties that made reference to mounds of squeezed citrus.

"It makes me think of Ground Zero, with the ash raining down."

She felt sometimes as if literature itself had been hijacked by the terrorists. Now all the references that didn't point to the crucifixion pointed to the terrorist attacks.

It was a ritual by now, walking her to her car, the drive out of town, the climb into the backseat. When there were condoms they used them, but when there weren't condoms or when they didn't use them, that was part of it, too. Rituals have an order that can be understood by outsiders, but not always a logic. There was a feeling among people during this period. Options were being taken down and stowed away. If you wanted something you had to grab.

The tape had sped up. That's how life felt. The news was trampling the daily struggles, instead of the other way around. You would be driving to buy groceries and a bulletin about anthrax poisoning or terrorist cells would come on the radio and you would get off the main road and sit on a side street until the panic passed and then go home. You could live without groceries.

But you couldn't, was the problem. On the way home from work she would force herself to detour and get two pieces of salmon at the supermarket for Phyllis to cook. When they sat down to eat she remembered something that had slipped her mind in the scurry of the day. An email from the one man she had dated in graduate school. He had gotten engaged. *To a northeast blueblood, would you believe.* She felt absurdly offended, as if he should have checked in with her first.

Thus began an odd downstepping chain of events. In December she got an early-morning call.

"He's dead."

Phyllis's favorite writer. He wasn't sixty.

"How?"

"Car accident. A fucking car accident. His daughter was in the car with him. She's okay." Then: "He's not finished with all the books he's supposed to write." Phyllis's voice trembled like an old woman's. "Sick of this shit—crap Alabama fascist—should just quit crap job and move back." She was crying openly now, incoherent. She would calm down in a bit, Sarah said. To herself she said, *She won't leave.* Meaning, *won't leave me.*

"It'll pass," Sarah said wanly.

In class, she caught herself not posing any serious opposition when students said things that were wrong. Let them be wrong: It wasn't going to kill them. "Hills Like White Elephants" wasn't about an abortion. Okay. A couple was just having an argument about the trains or drinks.

One afternoon, she felt sleepy in her office and took a walk by the new dorms to wake up. On a bench in front of a man-made lake, a man and a woman sat with their arms around each other.

Ron and Cassandra.

She found a note in her campus mailbox. The arrangements were made; Ron was shipping off for Afghanistan.

A turn of the kaleidoscope, and all the colored flecks fell into another arrangement.

Before Christmas, Tom took her to New Orleans. They drove down and went to Napoleon House, Commander's Palace, Galatoire's. Late at night, drinking daiquiris from foot-long plastic cups, they walked down Bourbon Street with its neon and vomit.

"Feels almost back to normal," Tom said.

In bed that night he said he had been thinking. He wasn't getting any younger, and what did she think of getting married?

She put her hand on his forehead. "Have you been drinking?"

"You know I've been drinking."

She woke in early morning to Tom's hands stroking her hips. She woke slowly, yielding with reluctance the desire to stay asleep. Her movements were passive; she let him turn her over on her stomach.

A scratching noise began, slowly first and then frantically.

"What is that?"

"Sounds like paws on particle board. Or claws."

He was panting irregularly, speeding up. "Probably a squirrel."

"Where?"

"Might've got himself caught between the wall and the insulation."

"Can he get out?" She pushed herself up on her elbows, and he slid out of her.

"Do you mind? We're doing something here."

"Is it going to die?"

Tom was up on his knees, holding his erection like a hotdog waiting for ketchup. "I don't know; it sounds like he's trapped. He'll probably starve to death. What am I supposed to do, break every fucking wall down and go looking for him?"

She started to get out of bed. "I don't want to do it now."

He had hold of her hair. "We don't always do what you want, Africa."

Afterwards, in the bathroom, she splashed water on her hurt face. How did he know about Ron? She debated for a while about what she had expected and went to lie on the sofa. This was just something she was doing because she wanted to lie on the sofa, she told herself. No one had ever hit her before. She didn't have any protocol for what to do next.

There was a line in *Gatsby* about Jordan Baker, Daisy Buchanan's friend who always sat next to her on the sofa with her white dress and powdery hands. Nick Carraway observes that she's a "clean, hard, limited" person. In the end, Nick hadn't married her.

Tom Sloan. Hard, limited. Not so clean.

Usually she didn't read the Fallen Warriors feature in the paper, but the face of the man in camouflage sitting at the wheel of a jeep caught her eye.

Huntsville Native Remembered For His Love of Reading

Mosul. Died from respiratory arrest. Found in his quarters with a book of stories by Hemingway. The article misspells the first name "Earnest."

She sat for a long time in her office with the newspaper page in front of her. So as to be rational.

🍸

The crowd inside The Confession Box is small but noisy, with very Irish-looking men playing the fiddle and bodhrán, and a black man in a knit cap on a pennywhistle. She orders a glass of Guinness (one couldn't hurt, could it?) and stands awkwardly in her bulky anorak next to the nearest table, where three women with shopping bags at their feet drink pints of Budweiser. On the other side of the street, the woman with the pillowcase is rooting in another bin. She sorts through trash the way women search the sale racks at department stores.

In this bar no one knows Tom Sloan or Ron Ajoloko or Sarah Foy.

Phyllis is coming up from Meath on a bus. Soon she'll be here, wanting to drink the miniature bottles of terrible wine.

Since moving back to Ireland, Phyllis has let her short hair grow out into shaggy layers. Sarah's surprised to see her in a wool sweater that's too big for her and a tweed skirt with low-heeled boots. She looks, Sarah realizes, like someone's mother.

"Would you believe I have sheep?" Phyllis says.

There are not a lot of things Sarah isn't willing to believe these days.

"You hope it's black," Phyllis says when they discuss the pregnancy.

"I hope it's Ron's."

"*I* hope it's black!" Phyllis laughs loudly. "Can I reject it if it's a little mushy pale Sloaney thing?"

The panic and doom fall on Sarah again. "The deal is, you can't reject it. You *said*."

Phyllis hugs her. "I'm just funnin' you. It's mine in any size or color. Even if it's sheep-shaped."

When the child is born with a full head of black hair and Ron's nose at the dour Our Lady's in Navan, she can see as she hands it to Phyllis that she's had the right baby for this mother.

"Look," Phyllis says, beaming. "My very own Alabama boy!"

Though he will be an Irish boy, reading Yeats and Joyce with Phyllis. Sarah vows she'll send *Gatsby* and Hemingway's *In Our Time* in the mail, to make sure they're on the bookshelves among the Irish writers. That much she can do for Ron.

౿

He's almost five now and loves winegums and Gaelic football and puddles and the goats. In the fall he'll attend the Christian Brothers school, where, Phyllis writes in an email accompanied by a photo attachment of a green-eyed, coffee-skinned boy, "with all these Nigerians, he doesn't stand out at all."

The Shift

The walls are white, the ceilings are white; the floors are cold white tiles shot through with black streaks. This room might once have been part of the hospital morgue, or at least this is what Tabitha tells Bev as they lower themselves onto bath towels brought from home. The Lamaze instructor's upright carriage, the black leotard she's wearing with a skirt as if this is a dance class rather than a class to teach you how to have a baby, her jutting clavicles—all this rebuffs the bulk of the women camped expectantly on the floor.

"Now it's heating up," Bev says. Each vertebra feels as if it's announcing its own form of ache. But if there's too much complaining from the pregnant contingent, Rupert might decide the class isn't worth the trouble. Bev and Rupert's four-year-old, Joan, was born the ordinary way, with knockout drugs. "This time I want an *experience*," Bev tells Tabitha, who is getting ready to have her first baby, and who is an aficionado of experiences.

The doctors aren't so gung-ho about these new participatory pregnancies, with the husband as coach rather than nervous appendage pacing the halls with a fistful of cigars. A story has been circulating about a woman who squatted to have her baby, another about a woman reputed to have given birth *underwater*. Behind one of the hospital's forbidding doors with their metal knobs and nameplates displaying words Bev and Tabitha have heard but don't know the exact meaning of—Hematology, Cytology, Oncology—a woman, skin shining with water and perspiration, might be half-submerged in a warm pool, a baby gliding out of her like a seal into the sea. Bev pictures a hot tub with underwater lights, like Hugh Hefner's at the Playboy mansion. It's Tabitha who pictures the sea.

Mostly Bev's glad that her first pregnancy is dim to her, the medications and admonitions confused in her mind with the protests and marches of '67 and '68. All that upheaval's over now; the country is settling down, and so is she. She and Rupert were living in Washington, D.C., then, in a two-room apartment Bev often spent whole days patrolling and tidying while Rupert was at work, designing among other, less exalted things the tracking light on the spaceship that landed on the moon. On their dining-room wall they have the laminated front page of the *Daily News* from July 21, 1969. Giving birth to Joan and the moon landing are tangled up with each other. Everyone—Rupert—was so worked up about the moon pod that she felt she had to try to get excited, too. "It's not a *pod*," Rupert had said. When Bev thinks of those days, the broadcast of Neil Armstrong's staticky voice is slotted in between Joan's infant bleats. But really the moon shrank to nothing beside the momentousness of giving birth. Of having something that large and loud come out of her body.

For Bev, Joan's birth is a blank bracketed at one end by the cold soak in the bed when her water broke and at the other by a yelp the nurse gave when she went to take the baby away and Bev clawed her arm. It was as if the hospital owned the baby and was giving Joan to Bev on consignment. They don't take away babies from their mothers so bossily anymore.

There's a low-level panic coursing through the air of this cold room, as if its inhabitants are about to be administered an exam on a different subject than the one for which they've studied. The feeling of not knowing, of being ill-prepared and of having to take the test anyway, is particularly acute in Bev. She didn't expect to be as anxious this time around. Given the choice, she would opt to go to sleep for the next few months and wake up when, or after, the baby is born. What do you do if you put down a baby for the night and it cries and cries? Is it normal for your firstborn to regress when you bring the new sibling home from the hospital? What to do if the baby refuses your nipple? The bottle? The formula? Now there are books and experts and conflicting opinions. A change has taken place. Tabitha says it's a bona fide paradigm shift. But it's not unusual for Tabitha to think there has been a paradigm shift.

Paradigm, schmaradigm, Rupert says. All it adds up to is that now people are less likely to say in public, *So I gave the kid a good wallop.*

So many people have shown up for the Lamaze class that the group will be split into two. The instructor tells Tabitha to stay in the seven o'clock, but Bev will have to be in the one at eight. Now they will only see each other in the parking lot when Tabitha and Alex are leaving, Bev and Rupert arriving. If they catch sight of each other when Tabitha's at one end of a row of cars and Bev's at the other, the two women contort themselves immediately into postures of suffering, as if the great burden of these children they're carrying has crippled them. They tilt their heads, their tongues lolling out of their mouths. Sometimes Bev tickles herself under the armpits, as if she's an ape. An ape in a cotton house dress.

"Now that's going too far," Tabitha says.

But other nights Tabitha is happy to be an ape, too. "When we get home, Alex is going to feed me a banana through the slats in my cage."

"Last time I did that, she bit me." Alex holds up a hand covered with pretend teeth-marks.

Before her pregnancy, Tabitha had a style characterized not so much by an effort to shape or alter her appearance as by a lack of exertion of any will at all. But maybe in reshaping her body so definitively, the pregnancy has given her ideas.

Ideas Tabitha and Alex—especially Alex—have at other times rejected. Bev has heard them speak about exploitation of women. She always pictures a large female nude made of melting ice falling from a height and smashing into a million shards in the street. Now Tabitha's thick brown hair is brushed and pinned down at her ears with two tortoiseshell combs. Her lips are coated a glossy pink, like a teenager's. And since this is an era of short dresses, even maternity dresses, it's discernible that Tabitha has gone to the trouble of shaving her legs.

"Tabitha's lost her pelt," Rupert says in the hospital elevator.

"That's not a nice thing to call it."

Rupert turns to her, a look of amusement on his face. "That was one hairy woman before."

Bev's hair is shoulder-length and frizzy, according to the style of the day for women of her age and political persuasions. She used to straighten it on the ironing board, with a towel and Rupert's help, when they were first married. '66, '67. Other times. In '61, ten years earlier, she'd been a cheerleader, head of the pep squad at high school, in a sweater with a blue bullhorn on it and the letters of her nickname—BINKY—sewn diagonally down the bullhorn.

She was not "Binky" Kaufmann anymore. She was Beverly Lake.

Maybe she should shave her legs, pay more attention to her wardrobe, go back to ironing her hair.

Rupert kisses the back of her neck. His tongue gives her a lick.

"You could take it easier on the hippie garb," he says as they step off the elevator.

Tabitha and Alex are avowed Communists; the only mark against them in the Lakes' book is that they have shown themselves to be a little too full of ideas and wine. But they are the antidote to Patti and Link Zorn, who live up the street from Bev and Rupert and organize block parties and dress their six-year-old in ruffled Polly Flinders dresses and go door-to-door for the Republican Party and the Methodists. Bev didn't ask Patti Zorn to join her consciousness-raising group. There's a pleasure in knowing that even though Patti Zorn wouldn't want to join, the five cars parked out in front of Bev and Rupert's house on Tuesday nights, the women moving across the yard in long skirts and peasant blouses, with casserole dishes or bottles of wine, trouble Patti Zorn. Group meetings stink of unrest, ferment. Maybe these women will post their poetry on telephone poles, declare monogamy a bankrupt idea, dress their children in androgynous overalls. All these ideas, in any case, have been floated.

Patti and Link are in the later Lamaze class, too. Bev is surprised to see Patti Zorn cross-legged on the floor, her belly straining at her blouse. The eyes are the best indicator of a person's mood. But Patti Zorn's eyes maintain the same implacability, even when she's smiling. Her mouth is the only feature of her face that expresses emotion. Link has the look of someone who was never meant to sit on a floor. He runs the Buster Brown store in Oyster Bay. You would think a shoe salesman would be comfortable close to the floor, the way Link is always having to kneel down and fit a foot into a shoe, measure feet, return shoes to boxes on the floor. It must be that Link doesn't like to be sitting on the floor with nothing to do. He has his legs bent in front of him, his hands clasped over his knees. It's impossible for Bev to imagine Link getting an erection. But it's also impossible for her to prevent herself from formulating a version of the events that brought these couples here. The erections (Bev counts seven men in the room), the pushing, the tangled bedclothes.

Before this pregnancy, Bev thought conceiving was a cinch. Joan had been, as Rupert said, *un accidente grande* after margaritas for dinner. But they had tried to plan this pregnancy. They figured out how many years they wanted between Joan and this baby, what season they wanted it to be born and then even got down to a preferred month. Then they tried and tried, and when it didn't happen, Bev began to wonder whether she really wanted another baby after all. Bev had planned to conceive in three months. But three months turned to five and then eight. One day she drove over to Hofstra University and got some literature about programs in social work. A few days later she went back and got an application.

She missed her next period. She was sitting on the toilet, reading about the program in social work, and she had a thought: *Shit it out before it becomes anything.* In the shower she pummeled her stomach. She went down to the kitchen and opened a can of beer and drank some as she walked back upstairs. The thought of getting drunk on Rupert's beer in the middle of the afternoon and ruining the baby, blood and the incomplete fetus falling out of her into the toilet—that thought woke her up. She had been feeling so sleepy. That she could do such a thing! Then she heard crying from the other room. Often after a nap, Joan thought there were pirates in the room and cringed in her little bed and described them to Bev—the ones who could swim under the ocean like fish and the ones out of whose mouths crabs and lobsters walked. Up early one morning, Joan had seen the squirming crabs and lobsters in the wooden traps on the lawn of the fishermen who lived next door.

Rupert always refers to the Zorns as Male Zorn and Female Zorn, as if they're aliens from a pod. While the instructor demonstrates panting (that's not the right word for it; Bev can never remember the right word), she steals furtive glances. Male Zorn, as Bev would have guessed, is showing no interest at all in what the instructor is saying. He might as well have a cartoon thought bubble drawn over his head with the words "tee time" in it. Female Zorn is paying polite attention, nodding but she isn't really listening, either. What would her cartoon bubble say? It would have an advertisement for soap in it. Showing up at Lamaze class, joining the citizens' committee to oppose the bridge the government wants to build across Long Island Sound from Connecticut—these are just gestures the Zorns are making, because the Zorns and even Tabitha and Alex, and Rupert and Bev, if she admits it to herself, participate in these social pantomimes so as to fit in with all the other young marrieds who live in Bayville. They are people who got shaken up by the Kennedy and King assassinations, but who had already settled down when the upheaval began to take place on the personal level. The new options for sex and drug experimentation, the casual defiance of authority that seemed to slouch in one day, the long hair on everyone is, for the people in this room, out of reach. Rupert now works for a company that designs anesthesia equipment, and only recently, belatedly, has he gone from clipping his curly hair close to letting it grow to touch his collar. *Fuck you, munitions industry,* Rupert says whenever anyone asks him about his former job with the government. But what is Bev trying to get at as she studies Female Zorn out of the corner of her eye? The difference between Patti Zorn and Bev is that Bev is expecting to go through with it, to learn the Lamaze and have her second baby with teeth clenched and without drugs. She'll squat like an animal if that's what's expected of her. She'll have her baby in a hot tub, if someone tells her that's where people are having babies now. Whereas Patti Zorn will report back to her circle of friends that she found the Lamaze method *interesting* but probably not right for her. Bev pictures Patti Zorn's second birth as placid and sanitary, Patti's face untroubled by contortions of pain. By getting involved with the women's movement, Bev has forfeited the right to a certain kind of refusal. She's no longer allowed the old inertia, though she's not sure whether it is more to her circle of friends or to herself or even to men that she has something to prove.

Rupert's taking notes on a brochure with a mechanical pencil. On the big day he'll be timing Bev's contractions. He has already gotten a stopwatch, in fact, from his father, a horologist of some renown. When Joan was born, Rupert was a textbook nervous-father-to-be. He grabbed Bev's prepacked suitcase without checking the clasp and dumped her belongings—nightie, slippers, makeup kit, toothbrush—all over the bedroom floor. He drove recklessly to the hospital. He said garbled things to the nurses in Admitting and had to ask around for antacid tablets. His hands shook. But now, with Lamaze, he is determined to be a helpful and effective husband. She hasn't wanted to disappoint him by telling him that truly, she would prefer to be given an epidural and told just to lie there, the way she did with Joan.

There's menace mixed in with Bev's feelings about this baby. As if this baby knows Bev once sat on the toilet and hoped it would slide out of her and be flushed.

ॐ

A few weeks after Petra is born, Bev's nursing on the sofa and almost dozing, a midmorning syrupy stupor. When the phone rings it's a feat for her to get up and work her way toward the kitchen with the baby and a blanket and her pendulous, leaking breasts.

"She lost it," Alex says. "It was born dead."

Bev thinks of the clump dripping into the toilet Petra might have been. She hoists her breasts back inside her blouse.

"Choked by the umbilical cord."

"I'll do something about the kids and then I'll come over."

But what to do with the kids? She would have to leave them with Female Zorn.

Bev shakes Joan out of bed and tells her to put on socks and shoes. As for the baby, well. She puts a hat on Petra and another blanket, as it's February, and she walks outside and up the wintry street. Snow is piled halfway up the fence posts in the yards, ice on the trees. Frozen puddles in the Zorns' driveway rip under her feet like seams.

There's a smugness that travels back and forth between Patti Zorn and Bev like an electrical current, each of them pleased with herself for tolerating the other. This is an occasion for Patti to tolerate Bev, who arrives on Patti's doorstep in hairy boots—fake hair—and a housedress and a blue quilted coat with a mandarin collar. Patti's newborn is a boy dressed in blue pajamas with baseball bats and balls and caps printed on them. Patti props open the front door with her foot for Bev.

"Could you take them for a while? I'd never ask but that it's an emergency."

"Of course." Patti of the implacable smile.

Bev hasn't been back to the hospital since Petra's birth. But the trembly panic she feels now feels like the same trembly panic she'd felt when she was admitted that day. That no one has thought to move Tabitha out of the maternity ward seems Neanderthal.

Where is Alex? In the cafeteria. "He was feeling faint, so they told him to eat something," Tabitha says. "He had a quarrel with some of them about being a vegetarian. The nurses told him he looks malnourished."

They don't talk about the baby yet. Bev thinks about Alex frowning at a Salisbury steak below them. Then about Rupert at work, making an anesthesia machine, whatever that entails. Bev hadn't thought to call to tell him about Tabitha or ask him to come home for the girls.

"Where are they?"

Bev realizes she's been wanting to ask Tabitha a version of the same question.

Where is *it?* Have they put it in a little coffin? The trash?

"Zorns'."

"You left them at Zorns'? They'll come back to you in uniform, with little epaulets on the shoulders."

Bev opens her mouth to laugh.

Tabitha's face tightens and creases with the effort of fighting back tears. "I wish I'd never done it at all, Bevs. Now I'm really done."

I

Petra had to get up early to pick up the irises. She started in with eyeliner before she remembered: Not even officers were allowed to wear makeup to Initiation. Though intended for symbolic purposes, the requirement had taken on other connotations. It was true Kappas wore a lot of makeup, but it was not true, as the rumor now went, that the ban on makeup at Initiation was the sorority's final opportunity to weed out the unattractive.

If she put it on now, she'd have to go to the trouble of taking it off later. She opted for just lipstick, then pulled a baseball cap down low on her forehead. It was unlikely she'd bump into anyone on the short walk from the dorm to her car, but there was always the chance. The path across the Quad was unprotected by trees and faced by dorm windows on three sides, so that anyone hurrying home in the previous night's formal clothes could be spotted and then turned into an object of speculation.

Her mother had called last night, late, to say Joan would be coming along. So there would be the food phobias to contend with, and maybe some tears about the married boyfriend. Too early to think about that. Petra didn't have a whopping hangover, just a fuzzy feeling that was a combination of too little sleep and maybe more Kahlua than she had intended.

She would have objected to saying that she hated her mother, but it was certainly the case that she didn't like her very much. She was embarrassed of a number of things. The frizzy permed hair, graying and dyed a too-bright brown. The sweatshirt and jeans she was likely to wear to the football game, while the other mothers would be in cardigans or boiled-wool jackets with blouses and skirts and leather boots. And the sweatshirt might have something like *Montauk* on it in cursive letters, with sand dunes and a seagull. Bev's white sneakers would end up getting muddy, and when she noticed how all the other mothers were dressed, she would sulk and ask Petra if this was a college or a country club. Ha ha.

A few months ago Petra's parents had called—one call, two extensions—to say her mother would be moving out of the house for a while. She would be renting a cottage at the other end of town until they worked out what to do about their marriage. Petra didn't think of marriage as something you *did something* about.

She had told people she was from the north shore of Long Island. True, but Bayville wasn't one of those Gatsby places with mansions perched on sea cliffs, just a ricky-racky summer resort town. A short boardwalk across from the public beach had Ralph's Pizza and Souvlaki Place and miniature golf and a batting cage that attracted derelict types. Petra had grown up on the other, more desirable end of town, this largely due to the funeral home and graveyard located there, but also an ostentatious seafood restaurant built on the stretch of beach just east of the funeral home. Without realizing it, she had always thought of the beach in her town, its foot-jabbing rocks rather than the standard sand, as somehow defective.

The phone call hadn't really surprised Petra, though she pretended she hadn't known there was trouble and cried into the phone and at one point also yelled. What was she crying and yelling about? Something having to do with her mother moving to the other side of town. The streets at that end of town had numbers instead of names, and the houses were small winterized beach cottages that hadn't been built as year-round residences. The result was a cluttered chaos. Cars were wedged every which way; awkward extensions were built on cottages that had enough land to add on; homemade sheds sprang up in backyards or in the narrow alleys. The tiny front yards were littered with toys and tricycles, and cramped dogs howled at each other from the closely packed backyards; there was on these streets the feel of a city block, noisy and unprivate.

It would have been bad enough for her mother to move to the cottage on the other side of town. But Joan had called Petra from their father's house (Petra thought of it as just their father's house now) two times to report that their father had slept out somewhere. Their father and Patti Zorn had gone out to dinner a few times. Mr. Zorn, Joan had heard, had gone west, to Nebraska.

Petra pictured her mother at the place on Third Street, with the mayhem and beer cans. There was a bar on the beach at the end of that street, a small converted house called Jimmy's Wharf, patronized mostly by townies. Joan's new boyfriend drank there. Also those angry old hippies, Tabitha and Alex Cotten. Why were they still angry, all these years later? Petra could respect them for being angry way back in the '60s; she had learned in her American Culture and Society class about the Student Non-Violent Coordinating Committee and the Freedom Riders. But now Tabitha and Alex drank Budweiser at Jimmy's Wharf and complained about Reaganomics and the Nuclear Age. "Nookular," Alex always said, and he said it a lot. He had showed up at Petra's high-school graduation party in a T-shirt with "Jimi Hendrix Slept with My Mother" written on it.

"Does that mean Jimi Hendrix is your father?" Petra had wanted to pour a drink on him.

He laughed at her joke; he was always thinking things she said were funny. "No, that means I have a little half-black half-brother!" He got up from the sofa and put his arm around her and hugged her. Some strange electrical charge went from him to her. She saw he was attracted to her and nearly overflowed with revulsion and pity for him.

Revulsion and pity. Petra wondered if they weren't so far from sexual attraction as she would have liked to think.

Everyone trying to figure out what to do with themselves. Petra didn't see the need for these contortions. You got out of bed in the morning and set yourself moving in your day, from the first thing to the next and the next. For instance, she was going to pick up the irises, bring them to the Kappa house, put them in vases. Other girls in her sorority would hang the sheets in the Initiation room. She would be needed to supervise. Then get the pledges lined up, perform the Initiation, deal with anybody who was freaked out (why did the ceremony always freak someone out?). Then eat, shower, change, makeup, parents, football game, Gregory. She wasn't a person who paused between one thing and the next. She was not for instance like Joan, who one day must have sat down with a plate of macaroni and cheese and started calorie-counting before she lifted her fork. Ever since, the topics of conversation between her and her mother had been Joan's weight, Joan's eating habits, do you think Joan is anorexic, how are we going to get Joan to eat?

You couldn't do that, you couldn't pay attention to every nuance and stage, or you would start going off the deep end. Petra remembered one of her high-school science teachers telling the class about the micro-organisms living in your eyebrows, a certain near-infinite number of parasites everyone had to live with, no matter how clean they made themselves. There were people who were immobilized by this information. Petra was not one of them.

⁊

Years ago Gregory's fraternity had instituted the tradition of setting up a bar on the field used for tailgating. The arrangement had become increasingly elaborate, so that now there was a giant Igloo cooler of pre-mixed Bloody Marys, bowls full of garnishes, bottles of Tabasco sauce and horseradish. People stood in the mud and gestured at each other with celery stalks. It also was starting to drizzle.

Finally Petra saw them, her father walking a little ahead of her mother with a camera held protectively in both hands. Sport coat and jeans, the sport coat flapping out behind him. Her mother wore white sneakers spattered with muck, her elbows crossed over her chest. She was wearing an anorak Petra recognized as one of her own from high school and blue jeans with creases. New jeans. The anorak's hood pulled up. Joan was several feet behind them, her head down, the sharp nose and cheeks and chin, a worried woodcut.

They stood in the drizzle, the four of them in a circle, each with a Bloody Mary in one hand and a stick of celery to stir it. Her father had gone to this college back in the '60's.

"Completely different! Even though so many buildings are exactly the same," Rupert said, pointing with his celery stick at dorms where he'd lived when he was a student.

"They didn't have women then," Bev said.

"Well, that would make all the difference."

Petra had seen photos of campus during her father's time. Though it had been an all-men's school, there were plenty of women in them. But the women seemed largely ornamental. She remembered the belted dresses and the flowers behind the ear or pinned to the women's collars. The way the men frozen by the camera were so often in poses that suggested they were steering the women.

The fraternity brothers working behind the bar—and this was incongruous, too, almost surreal, with the long view of the football field and the Quad's Gothic towers as background, where the bottles lined up behind a bar should be—were singing, very low, so that it was hard to catch the lyrics, a song that must be one of the fraternity songs, that only the brothers know.

did her did her good
pushed it up her spine

A loud burst of noise and clapping, with all the brothers bent over behind the bar to get more cups and ice suddenly straightening for the crescendo

and Drink, Drink, Drink
and Drunk, Drunk, Drunk!

Startled laughter from the parents assembled in front of the bar, toasting with plastic cups of Bloody Mary in the drizzle and mud.

Petra thought she must be hearing incorrectly. The business about the spine must be her own invention. It had to do with Joan, who had taken off her anorak and draped it over her arm.

"Put that back on. You'll freeze to death," Petra said.

"How far is it around campus?" Joan said. "I might go for a run." The rain made the loose shirt cling to her. It was upsetting to look at the angles and bones.

Petra ignored the question and scouted for her little sister in the sorority, Courtney from Texas, whose parents were dressed in similar wool blazers. One of Gregory's friends kept a framed photo of the Reagans, skinny Nancy in a yellow dress that always made Petra think of a sliver of butter.

"I have to use the bathroom," Joan said.

Petra thought about going with her and giving her a good talking-to.

The one on the second floor of Jarvis Towers, a converted men's room with walled-up urinals, was where they found her, unconscious.

II

Joan must have been seven or eight when she rounded the corner to Petra's bedroom and saw her mother and Tabitha together. The embrace alone would hardly have registered—this was a home where women embraced women, men embraced women, children were swung off the ground and into the arms of parents and their friends. In fact Tabitha, who had no children of her own, had been a favorite of Bev's daughters, She'd swung them off the ground in airplane circles and held Petra upside down by her ankles until she screamed with laughter. Many times, when she was a girl, Joan had sat on the top stair step and listened to her mother's consciousness-raising group talk and clink glasses. As the evening progressed, there would be crying, and crying often preceded hugging. But the way her mother and Tabitha Cotten were embracing wasn't anything Joan had seen before. Even a child can see a difference between a consolatory hug and a passionate embrace.

"You wouldn't have to go," Tabitha said.

"I'd stay here?"

They stood in piles and piles of Petra's toys and shoes and looked at each other while Joan watched them from the hallway. There must have been some electrical charge that signaled to Joan that life was going to change, dramatically and soon. It could not have been just those words, even though the way Bev said them would have made clear to anyone, even an eight-year-old, that Bev couldn't stay.

But if not here, where?

"Petra has something of the Zorn in her, eh?" This from Tabitha. The women weren't embracing anymore. They were stepping over toys and picking them up and looking at them and letting them drop back down to the floor. Four years old, and already Petra owned too many things. She was becoming a collector: Dolls of Many Nations, Weebles, Fisher-Price toys, Barbies. Joan at that age had been a collector of bottle caps, but that ended abruptly when she decided to wash her bottle caps by soaking them in a jar of water and turned them rusty.

Something of the Zorn in her. That had not made sense to Joan, then. Oh, certainly the Zorns might have been members of another species. The Zorns went to the Methodist church on Sunday mornings. A crèche appeared on their front lawn early in the Christmas season. Joan and Petra could not even have identified the figures in the tableau, and Petra only got more confused when informed by Female Zorn that the baby in the manger had the same name as the one hanging from the cross. And why was he hanging from the cross? And what were our sins?

Petra came home from playing with the Zorn kids and reported that they had an "Advance" calendar with one flap you opened each day to get closer to Jesus. They served *chops* for dinner, and Female Zorn (*Mrs. Zorn,* Petra corrected her mother) wore an apron to serve the food, and before they ate Mr. Zorn bowed his head and said something very quickly that began *Dear heavenly father.* There was a shaggy cover on the toilet seat, and a lot of the rooms had TVs. A *lot,* Petra repeated, and demanded to know why in houses such as theirs and Tabitha and Alex's there were none.

Bev held a Barbie in one hand and a Doll of Many Nations in the other. "Joan'll be easier," she said to Tabitha.

"Joan'll be *with* you."

At the time, Joan didn't know what Tabitha's remark meant. She didn't know the distinction between literal and figurative being *with.* She was surprised when her father told her that her mother had gone off to California to spend her thirtieth birthday on her own.

☙

The black threads in the white tiled floors look to Joan like streaks of dirt. But of course hospitals have to be clean. It's a rule. As she watches the TV with the sound off, she thinks about Petra having *something of the Zorn* in her, like yeast in bread.

Commercials seem to be the main fare of television. Dancing foam bubbles, kids flipping on skateboards, soda waterfalls, anthropomorphic dogs. It's tiring. TVs in hospital rooms always seem to be mounted too high, in the corners near the ceiling. She doesn't like the feeling of the TV looking down at her and wishes someone would come to turn it off. Outside, Albany is drizzling. No, places don't drizzle. She can't remember when she last ate, though she has very specific images, very specific yearnings, for particular foods in particular containers. A tuna casserole of her mother's in a white-and-blue CorningWare dish. Cauliflower with melted cheese poured over it as if the head is a human head and the melted cheese a gag someone is playing. The cauliflower has to be served in a deep and stylish white bowl decorated around the rim with what look like pencil drawings of varieties of mushrooms. She remembers the bowl from her childhood, and she remembers one day finding new red Jell-O in the bowl in the refrigerator, and of being so excited by it that she knelt in front of the open refrigerator and stabbed at the Jell-O with her hands.

For years she has kept a little blue diary of her food rules and violations.

Eamon is supposed to arrive soon, and then her mother and sister sometime after that. She pictures them running into each other in the white corridor and falling into each other's arms the way relatives do in times of crisis. The family resemblance between her mother and her would be immediately apparent to Eamon.

She doesn't know, anymore, whether she looks like Petra.

It was chewable.

This is what Joan thinks Eamon is saying.

"I have to go back to the store, honey. Nuala thinks that's where I am."

His upper lip is swollen to the size of a duck's bill. "I can't kiss you," he says.

Doesn't want to, she thinks. Everything inside and outside her is hazy, washed with that wash painters brush on canvases to prep them.

It was *tubal.* That's what he's saying. Eamon's Irish accent mashes it into *chewable.* She has blown out one of her ovaries. The little Eamon that couldn't. The little Joan. She thinks she would like to be so small her whole body could fit inside a tube.

"I'll kiss your forehead," Eamon says.

Far-id, is how he says it.

"Not if I kiss yours first." One of the umpteen little jokes they laugh at now because it reminds them that they're *them,* Joan-and-Eamon, two people in love with each other who can't be together yet.

The problem with his mouth is probably stress-related. He shrugs. Americans have "stress-related problems." He just has an infection, from ordinary germs.

She liked everything about his mouth from the moment she met him when she was hired at the health-food store. Once she told him about the dream she always had of people with crabs and lobsters walking out of their mouths with pincers open. He didn't analyze it and make her seem psycho, the way her mother would have.

The Guinness will give you wild dreams if you drink too much of it.

They'd had a lot to drink one afternoon.

"I'll go now," he says from the doorway of her room.

"You have 'Organic' stickers all over your back."

He has just two of the yellow stickers on his back. But she's trying to alter the mood of their meeting in such a way that it'll seem like only one small moment in a sequence of events in her and Eamon's future life together, rather than the final scene. "I'll go now" is a line from a final scene. But the final scene couldn't be him with a duck-bill mouth and organic stickers stuck to his Made in China acrylic sweater.

"Go to the dentist," she says. But he won't, unless the pain gets unbearable. He's in America illegally and has no health insurance.

When he has been gone a little while she tries to call up the exact exchange that took place between them. Maybe it's a side effect of the anesthesia that she can't.

Her mother arrives carrying flowers wrapped in lavender tissue. Tabitha has books. Petra isn't with them.

"I didn't even think you *had* a *boyfriend,*" Bev says, touching Joan's face and then her hands. This is still the joking phase, before the doctor comes in and asks Bev and Joan questions. Do they know Joan's cervix is shaped like a coxcomb? Did Bev take any pills while pregnant with Joan? If so, what were they for?

"I have no idea what my daughter's cervix is shaped like," Bev says. A good moment of combined levity and dignity. There has not been a lot of dignity of late.

"Draw the *regular* cervix," Tabitha says. "We're not even sure what the regular one looks like."

Bev says yes, she remembers the doctor giving her pills while she was pregnant with Joan. "I think to prevent miscarriage."

"Had you ever had a miscarriage?" the doctor asks.

"No."

"She's probably a DES daughter," the doctor says.

Joan doesn't like the idea of being an anything daughter. She wills an interest in the books Tabitha has brought, one called *Black Like Me* by a white man in the South who painted himself, in a way not explained to Joan's satisfaction, black, and experienced the prejudice of white people firsthand. Also *Survival in Auschwitz*, which kept Tabitha distracted "when I was going through some very tough stuff," though she doesn't elaborate. She has gained weight since Joan last saw her and is wearing a batiked Indian cotton dress that wafts around her body. Joan doesn't ask about Tabitha's tough stuff because she doesn't want them to ask probing questions about Eamon, who in addition to the dental and immigration problems has a wife and a baby.

"I ran into a man in the gift shop who asked if I was your mother. Was that him?"

"It doesn't matter." Joan pictures her ovary bursting. Not the bursting of the space shuttle with the astronauts in it. Not a disaster.

III

In Petra and Gregory's guest bathroom, Bev sits on the closed toilet seat to change her stockings. Already her first pair is laddered with runs. Why did she get control top? She takes hold of the elastic waistband and pulls with both hands. Stretch them out—make them fit her, rather than the other way around. Black stockings, and with her fists inside them she has black fists.

A rap on the door. "You okay, Bevs?"

She doesn't answer. She wants to smoke a joint, but she can't get the bathroom window to open. If Petra smelled it she'd go berserk.

The rapping's more insistent now. "Are you in there? Are you okay?"

"I'm okay."

She's not sure how she'll get through the rest of this day. The only way she has been able to manage so far is going back and back in her life, rewinding. Going forward is dangerous.

So, back.

The party had devolved into a modest sort of pre-orgy, with permission given—called out over the music, with wineglasses raised by various people around Tabitha and Alex's living room—for a husband to kiss a person who wasn't his wife, or for certain kinds of groping to take place in the context of slow dancing. A group of people was already bumping and grinding in the middle of the living room, so it was good that these new laws were declared. A pair of arms came in from behind and grasped Bev around her waist. The grassy smell told her it was Alex. Grass as in marijuana, but Alex also always smelled vaguely of fresh-cut grass, too, as if he'd just finished mowing a lawn. The funny thing was that Alex and Tabitha's house didn't have a lawn. It was one of a tightly packed block of winterized beach houses that didn't have enough property for a lawn. Even if it had, the soil was sandy and thin, not the right kind of soil.

He dug his hands in under her breasts, which had stayed big even after weaning Petra. She didn't know how she felt about Alex's hands dug in like that, but she continued shimmying gamely. From the other side of the room, Tabitha smiled at her and rolled her eyes. She was boogeying unencumbered, arms in the air. This was the era of disco. In fact, Rupert had, in very un-Rupertlike fashion, presented himself to Bev in a white suit like Travolta's in *Saturday Night Fever*.

When the song changed, Bev boogeyed away from Alex. She and Tabitha met under a Calder-like mobile hung in a corner.

"Don't let that get tangled in your hair," Tabitha said. "That's happened to me."

"So the rules have changed," Bev said. She was feeling bold and also a little angry about Alex having danced with her from behind, without ever making eye contact.

"He's practicing pollinating. He wants to try for a baby again."

"Disco Inferno" started playing, and both of them began side-stepping and snapping their fingers while they talked. Bev looked over and saw Rupert hand-feeding a woman something.

Tabitha took Bev's arm and steered her into the foyer. Women had hung their purses and sweaters on a coatrack.

"You and me'd have a baby," Tabitha said. "That's what I wish."

It was an idea so out of bounds at the time that Bev couldn't think of how to respond. She decided make a joke.

"I suppose you'd be the father, and I'd have to do all the tough stuff."

Tabitha put her arm around Bev. Her patchouli-scented hair fell on Bev's shoulder. "We'd both be the mothers, both the two of us, one, two."

"My eggs are too old," Bev said.

"And mine are bad. Or something is. Maybe Alex's."

It might have been the loud music that made Bev not realize that Tabitha had been slurring.

"It was just the umbilical cord. The birth went wrong—I bet you could have another baby." She stroked Tabitha's hair. The gesture made her feel like Tabitha's mother, and the room with the people and music in it tilted and reeled for a moment before it righted itself.

"I don't feel so well," Tabitha said.

"Like you might be sick?"

Tabitha nodded, and Bev hurried her to the bathroom and shut the door behind them. It was okay—Tabitha knelt down just in time, and Bev held her hair until she was finished.

They were both already over thirty then. They wanted to try psychedelic mushrooms; they wanted to leave their husbands. All their friends wanted to try psychedelic mushrooms and leave their husbands. But that Tabitha wanted them to mother a baby together: that was new. Women didn't have babies with each other in those days. As always, she had been behind Tabitha in anticipating the shift.

Just as Bev gets the stockings up, she has to pee. She works the stockings down, opens the lid again, and sits.

Nothing. It's been like this all week: having to go desperately when she's nowhere near a toilet and not having to go at all when she has the opportunity.

Shit it out before it becomes anything.

How has she forgotten that? The Hofstra application on her dresser. Her wish for a quick red clump in the toilet, out and gone.

Petra's guest bathroom has black-and-white photos on the wall facing the toilet, so that you're looking at solemn-faced people posing for their portraits while you're on the can. Who are they? Swarthy and mysterious Italians who look like Gregory. Then Bev recognizes Rupert's family, his grandparents and aunts and parents in a garden.

There's five-year-old Rupert in the middle, looking disappointed as he holds the reins of a rocking horse.

There are no photos of Bev's family.

What had Joan done to herself in bathrooms? Not this one, of course. Petra and Gregory have only just finished their renovations on this house.

The vomiting and subterfuge. All that illness.

The implacable face in the coffin might have been Patti Zorn's but for the sharp bones in the cheeks, which were rouged, her eyelids brushed with silvery-blue eyeshadow. Wasn't it odd that it was called eyeshadow when what you were trying to do was emphasize the eyes? The lips were painted a mulberry color that Joan wouldn't have chosen even as a third or fourth choice. Petra had done it herself, with her own cosmetics but with different brushes and spongy wedges. The lipstick, after its one important use: would it have been thrown away?

Bev touched the hands but not the face.

It hadn't been one thing. There were numerous stress points; you couldn't say that the blown-out fallopian tube or Bev and Rupert's divorce or her moving in with Tabitha, by themselves, had been the cause. The disappearing Irishman. Other things.

She didn't think Joan had ever disapproved of Tabitha. Joan had not been judgmental.

She holds her face up to the mirror and darkens the mouth with lipstick. She talks to the face.

"Petra is what you have now."

She's repeating what Tabitha said to her, to get herself used to the sound of it.

The Yak Pants

Midday at the office. Lunchish. Penelope's parked on my desk, chewing the ends of my pencils. I haven't told her the peeve I have about that. Penelope makes her own rules.

"You taking lunch?"

I never take lunch. At midday I sit on my hands at my desk and smell other people's lunches. I smell Marcia's lunch and Ryan's lunch and Tamika's lunch.

Tamika's lunches smell like starch and oil. If calories had a smell, that would be the smell of Tamika's lunch.

"You should take lunch," Penelope says. "Sometimes I like to go have the mini–Buddha Specialty Salad at Yokimo's. They give you daikons for the eyes. I get the vino in the little decanters."

"I don't know anything about that." I pretend to myself I am scowling because of "daikons." I pretend I am scowling over "vino." Really I am scowling over, more generally, lunches. Who does she think she is, Miss Ass-on-My-Desk? With her daikons and vino? In the middle of the day? For no particular occasion?

"And with the decanters? You order the sampler and they bring you six on a tray with just a few tablespoons of vino in each, so you're not loopy after lunch. I would never want to imply I come back from lunch loopy, as I take this job seriously."

The truth is I know exactly the decanters she's talking about. Lunches like that add up to money I can't spare. Last year Ma had a stomach-stapling operation that got botched. Now there's leakage, she needs iron infusions, her body cavities have been breached. If there is one thing you want to completely not think about, it's your mother's body cavities being breached.

"I am perfectly a-okay with whatever I can scrounge up here. I have no need for *decanters*, especially when it's only *Tuesday*."

Penelope's turning over the snow globe my mother sent me from the city. The blizzard is soot gray. "Stop fixating on decanters, Angela, you're creeping me out."

"You're the one who brought it up." I don't say I'm on edge because my mother needs an operation or her shit cavity'll leak into her food cavity. I don't say I feel guilty she turned into as she says an *obosity* from putting me through school via a sedentary desk job of the very type I now work and eating takeout mac'n'beef platters for lunch every day. I don't say that at college I started hating the turquoise boxes sent to classmates in which arrived not just poundages of jewelry but sterling silver candle snuffers, hip flasks, tie clasps, cufflinks, ice buckets, and letter openers that could have worked perfectly as little stabbing knives. The stunt was to drop objects off dorm balconies. Leather ottomans, mallets from mallet sports, rains of shoes made from lizard skins and worn *once*. Was there some kind of rulebook for this stuff? They dropped punch bowls, decanters, Champagne glasses. Thak-splat, a family heirloom splintering in a jillion pieces in the courtyard below. Oh, those crazy college kids, with our cummerbunds and gin-and-tonic midmornings. I faked it pretty good then, lockjaw accent and peau de soie shoes.

"You're pretty small, aren't you?" Penelope says. "You probably don't eat much."

It's true about not eating much, which is my sore spot, which is when Penelope, who is an exceedingly small woman to the point where her head looks too big for her body, tells me she has some excellently cut clothing from her sister that doesn't fit her that she would be much obliged if I would try on, lest the designer garments go to waste.

"I don't wear a two or zero," I say.

"Fizzlesticks," Penelope says. "You can't be any bigger than my pinky finger!"

"I am much bigger than your pinky finger! In fact, I am in the vicinity of an Italian sausage that has busted through its casing and is grotesquely poking out in big marbled gelatinous adipose blobs with little extra horns of it sticking out even further like suet crullers hung from a tree for the squirrels and birds to eat."

"That is so funny," Penelope says. "Because on any given day I am an oleaginous pile of flesh spilling out of this wispy peasant blouse and these so-called skinny jeans and these riding boots I insist upon wearing even though I am literally treading flab and offending everyone in the vicinity with my leaking blubber."

Because I am the larger of the two of us, it's incumbent upon me to reassure her.

"Don't even try to reassure me," she says. "It's my fault that my fat's so unevenly distributed that I can't fit into these perfectly good designer clothes worn maybe once that my sister sent me and so I'm passing them along to you in the hopes of finding a perfect fit, which will hopefully fingers and toes crossed be you. Sometime, Angela, I insist it, we must must must go for lunch and order six decanters each and the Buddha Specialty Salad with extra daikons."

◌

I'm quartering a head of iceberg when a thak-splat shakes my porch. It's the sack of clothes from Penelope's sister, all tied up with a gold ribbon and an environmentally positive green one that together are a Penelope hallmark. Also a computer note in calligraphic font saying she hopes I can like and appreciate the youthlike wisdom of her sister's sartorial choices. These include, among other things, yak-hair pants and several wispy hemp *blusas* of the peasant variety Penelope favors and what looks like a belted raincoat designed for a Barbie doll that I can't even get my finger through the sleeve of, much less my arm. I try and it gets stuck and I have to get Mike to cut it off with scissors so it's ruined.

Mike says, "Let's not get all involved in this business right before dinner." Already I'm getting undressed.

"There is never any circumstance imaginable under which any woman would feel good or for that matter look good wearing a tiny, puny pair of yak-hair pants," Mike's saying. "Also, that is the hide of a formerly live animal, which last I checked is contra to your value system." This is just his lame attempt to distract me from making the low screaming noise in my throat as I try to get the yak pants over the lower parts of myself.

"Maybe you should instead try one of the *blusas*," Mike says. "Though in truth I find them somewhat unappealingly Penelope-like."

"It's not that they're Penelope-like, it's that they're thinperson-like, and I'm not currently in that category, what with having big marbled gelatinous blobs of genetically inherited suet crullers poking out everywhere!"

Then Mike's tearing the yak pants out of my hands, and I'm screaming in my not-so-quiet voice, and Mike's saying, "What's gotten into you? What does it matter if you can't fit into Penelope's sister's teensy *blusas?*" Which is how I end up telling him over a glass of our cheap jug wine about Penelope's lunches out with her little decanters of vino and how by offering me these twos and zeros she claims are her sister's but I'm beginning to suspect are her own castoffs she's duped me and now I'm going to have to eat quartered iceberg for the next eighteen years to prove to her I appreciate her generosity; also that I have willpower.

"One thing I am going to do right now is invite that Penelope over here and have her tell you that under no circumstances imaginable did she intend to insult or humiliate you by generously offering you her sister's or whoever's they are yak pants." Mike went for the old trick of putting his arm around me, as if to say, "I love and accept you, even in your grotesque state of utter corpulence" (he would call me *zaftig*), but I grabbed his wrist and prevented him. I tried to put the kibosh on his plan, but he rang Penelope anyway. She was at exercise class, Abel said. However, *he* would love to come by for a drink.

When Abel saw the yak pants and *blusas* all over my living room he got senatorially calm and said, "One thing you have to understand about Penelope and her sister is they have long been the recipients of many goods and services, in the form of being showered with gifts from their parents, who are shall I say endowed with a seemingly infinite supply of resources. This showering can grow quite unwieldy after a while, in the form of being drowned in yak pants, peasanty *blusas*, the raincoat to which you refer with some degree of animosity, etcetera."

"So they need to throw things off balconies."

Abel nodded yes and no. "Well, that's an immature way to manage one's plenteousness. The more enlightened way is to bestow it as gifts upon others, as is the case with Exhibit A," he said, pointing at the piles of yak pants and the little hacked raincoat. "You see, this is just her way of sharing her plenteousness with you."

Okay, I said. Tell Penelope thank you a thousand times for these pants and also the little grosgrain belts I could wear as headbands. Hail these wispy peasanty *blusas* that do not in any way fit across my torso. These are gifts of plenteousness, and I will do right by them.

I got down on the floor and picked up each pair of yak pants and each wispy *blusa* and folded them into nice piles and I was senatorially calm and Mike and Abel traded sports stats while I carried my gifts up to my room and set them down next to my computer.

An e-mail from my mother dinged in: *Not to get too graphic about it lovie but the contents of the various cavities have been commingling in ways according to the doctor that are inadvisable. don't shit where you eat well ha tell that to my stomach. this is such a strange age lovie with being able to get hi-tech operations but then maybe me just dying in the end anyway with something so plebe as a perforated bowel or sepsis. give my love to mike.*

It just didn't seem fair, Penelope with all that plenteousness and Ma suffering.

The surgery was elective, so insurance doesn't want to hear about her leaking bowels. After all, as my Ma says, who does?

One month later.

"Ooh, girl," Tamika said. "Them hairy pants are walking along shoutin' something in the ear of the world!"

Tamika was all in orange, wig and everything. She was even chewing something orange. I am not saying I have anything against monochromatism. However. If Tamika says any of your sartorial choices is shoutin' in the ear of the world, that is not generally a good thing. The situation is that (without starting a race war here) Tamika has an aesthetic which is a lot blacker than mine, which is WASP-y down to the bony clavicles poking out of evening gowns and claw hands dripping with signet rings and rickety thin legs from golf and tennis and also the prominent cords in the neck. Whereas Tamika thinks a woman looks good with a back end like a peach and a cleft between the breasts that you could lose a purse in.

I had managed at that point, just, to work my way into the yak pants along with the most forgiving of the *blusas*. I could manage except for sitting down. Instead I leaned against the wall to read my files, and if I needed to send an email I stood at my desk and angled forward. Only thing was, if I dropped something on the floor it had to stay there. So far I had dropped a pencil, a paper clip, and my last piece of gum, which fell out of my hand on the way to my mouth.

You'd be surprised by the degree of animus you can generate toward a coworker who walks into your office and bends over just like that in her own yak pants, with no visible strain, and retrieves your last piece of gum.

"Want to go to lunch? I'll buy."

Did I want to go to lunch? Had I subsisted on nothing but tea, iceberg lettuce, and giant gulps of air for days on end? Would I have given anything for a decanter of vino and the two half-moon slices of daikon?

The thing was: I couldn't sit at a restaurant unless I undid the pants, and undoing the pants would mean defeat. Plus the pants made Penelope my buddy, and making Penelope my buddy might eventually and hopefully not too long in the future yield a check paid to the order of Ma for the repair of one leaking bowel.

I would go to lunch. I wouldn't undo the pants. I would assume a seated position in a dignified manner. Yak pants would not triumph. Ma's bowel would triumph. I would triumph.

Penelope drives a sporty car with leather interior and a suede infant seat in back. She adopted a baby from overseas and recommends it. In fact she recommends it all the time.

"We could help you and Mike with the paperwork and bureaucratic ding-dong, which believe *me is* a major headache that could mostly be averted by knowledgeable friends." She takes her hand off the gearshift and pets my yak leg.

"I don't really think I'm the mothering type. For one thing I am having trouble just helping out *my* mother, who is in the throes of a negative health situation." A lot of people don't like to hear anything about stomach stapling, and who's to blame them? Also a lot of people have trouble feeling empathy toward people who get gastric bypasses. For instance, the waitresses at The Crawfish Boil used to give Ma such a look of contempt when she ordered the Fried Fresh Fish Pile Platter with a side of mayo-dipped onion chunks instead of the boiled crawfish. The breaking point came when they started skimping on the coleslaw and secretly making her soda a diet. Was Penelope this judging kind of person? Would someone who wore the headdress and body art of her adopted child's native land for thirteen months straight to help the child acculturate be this judging kind of person?

I thought not.

"Do you think deep down you don't want to have a baby because you want to not be one of those women like your mother who degrade into being overweight with the large jugular milking breasts and the extra post-baby stomach, hip, and thigh blubber?"

I say I don't think the adjectival form of "jug" is "jugular."

"Because you don't want to just be a ginormous machine that churns out the baby and then passes into totally broken-down obsolescence like those computers that used to take up an entire room?" Penelope's tearing along at a pretty good clip. I'm doing that involuntary nervous-passenger behavior where I paste my back to the seat and stomp a nonexistent brake, which strains the yak pants.

"Actually I don't like babies."

Penelope pulls into a parking space and gives me a dark look. "You don't do lunches, you don't like babies. Abel tells me he and Mike had to move heaven and earth to get you to try on those yak pants—and now look at you strutting your stuff! You never know, I may even convince you to order the mini–Buddha Salad and the decanter sampler yet! Which might mean, not long behind it, a nice little infant from one of the catastrophic-droughty and wracked-by-internal-conflict parts of the world!"

I don't know where she got her info about moving heaven and earth when I was the full impetus behind wearing the yak pants. Mike would have been much happier if the yak pants and I never made each other's acquaintance. There are some people who live in a particular way, and hell be damned if you don't live the way they do and adopt the baby from a droughty country because you prioritize helping your mother's bowel. And you can come to resent the way certain people can even eat occasionally and still have the narrowest ass at work. I am speaking of one group of people, and that is the balcony-throwers, the disseminators of multiple pairs of yak pants and *blusas* and, while I am mentioning it, also the purchasers of a set of underweight goats and a dirt-floored hut for the backyard and some malarial-looking hangers-on to help the baby from overseas with the transition (I saw photos in Penelope's cubicle, with a sheet draped over the privet hedge in the background so as not to distract from the scene of deprivation with conventional greenery).

At Yokimo's, Penelope and the headwaiter do a quick sideways bow that's a new one on me and we're seated at one of the high tables I thought you could only get if you had special connections, which it dawns on me for the first time, duh, Penelope must have.

"Listen, Anj," Penelope says.

The elevated tables mean I could sort of sit-stand, one foot on the floor, one cheek on the chair.

"You just order whatever you want, like if you want twelve decanters instead of six that's fine with me and/or the Buddha Specialty Kilimanjaro which is a conical sort of volcano of stacked beef that comes with an excellent umeboshi sauce for lava and lychee nuts for lava rock. Consider it on mi casa, amiga."

Just the words "stacked beef" all by themselves without the food they represented made the pants tighter.

"What are you getting, Penel?" We were chums now, Anj and Penel, Penel and Anj.

"I often tell them to have the chef whip up whatever inspires him. Just make sure it's sculptural, I say, since that's el nombre del game-o."

Having no idea what she was talking about, I pretended I knew exactly what she was talking about, to the point of throwing some Spanish expressions into my own conversation. A fish plate she insisted I get arrived (¡muchas gracias!) and a noodle plate (¡bueno!) and a rice plate and the stacked beef volcano with umeboshi and lychee (¡basta!). A nice waiter came by and Penelope insisted on a splurge just this once and gave him a wink that led him to whip out a long fork and feed me. Of course I had heard about this, but money is always the issue.

"No hay simpatico to turn down hospitality," Penelope said, reminding me how it was the job of me and other less-fortunates like me to relieve her of her plenteousness—much as her overseas baby could siphon off some and make our own lives more enriched while simultaneously unburdening Penelope of her glut.

I still couldn't figure out the right way to bring up how I needed money for Ma's bowel. I kept eating. The nice waiter nodded gubernatorially and went for the stacked beef and lychees and put an umeboshi smear under my nose. "Now feed some to Penel," I said. I was woozy on noodles and wine the waiter poured from each of the decanters into a wide straw he stuck in my mouth for which I understood Penelope had paid even more extra.

Two towers made from a moist and pale radish teetering in translucent slices, in grouped sections held together by green reeds tied in bows made from celery ribs, appeared in front of Penelope.

"La pièce de résistance." But instead of digging in, she blew at it. She blew again, and when it didn't blow down she nudged the structure with a finger, and it toppled into a sad "L" on the plate. "Good, delicious, great meal, thank you, Yokimo! (Even though his name's not actually

Yokimo, they all let me call them that)," she said. Then she stood to go. The difference between her and me as we stepped away from the table was her yak pants stayed intact and mine split.

"The thing about your *plenteousness*, Penelope." I was speaking through shut teeth and trying also to hold my pants shut. Not just because I was angry but because the plan for me was never to open my mouth again, so that food wouldn't slip in from someplace I didn't ask for like that waiter's fork. I was ramping up toward what Mike would have called one of my threshing bonanzas, getting ready to slash everything in sight.

She held up a hand. "Calm down while I pay and get a mint."

I grabbed a napkin off a table and unfolded it to cover the parts of my flesh poking out from behind the yak and not doing anything aesthetically desirable for the yak or me. How had I gotten so sidetracked and let Penelope stuff me like a goose when I was supposed to be lobbying for Ma's bowel? What was I doing eating at a time like this? No one wants to think of herself as a giant lump made of lard being wheeled into the O.R. by a doctor with six-pack abs under his scrubs. Just imagine his disdain at having to scalpel his way through all the fatty tissue to staple that person's stomach shut.

On the way back in the car it was clear that the sight of me, even covered with a napkin, offended Penelope and her whole sense of how the disbursement of plenteousness was supposed to work. Meaning the recipients aren't supposed to be disgusting, they're not supposed to bust out of their yak pants in public. I knew now it wouldn't make things better (in fact, a whole lot worse) if anyone was to mention at this point Ma's bowel.

I asked Penelope if she wouldn't mind dropping me off at my apartment instead of work so I could change. Actually, I had no intention of returning to work and letting Tamika infer about the yak pants getting the best of me.

❧

Another few months later.

I have been seeking alternative ways to pay for Ma's negative health situation. The ways I am finding are what some people such as maybe

Tamika would call *just tryin' to make it*. It's the old question about whether it's okay to steal a loaf of bread if your kid is starving. Substitute *sell company property on eBay* for the loaf of bread and *your Ma's leaking bowels* for your kid is starving. I say an unqualified yes. I sleep well at night.

There's a lot of property in the office sitting around totally underutilized, and it's only that stuff I sell. In addition, Penelope had about seventy silver rattles and spoons in turquoise boxes her friends sent from all over to congratulate her for adopting her baby from the war-torn nation. Not needing seventy rattles and spoons for one little baby who was getting along perfectly well in her dirt-floored hut and eating with her hands whatever Penelope set on the floor and using for a rattle a hollowed-out gourd filled with BBs, Penelope had planned to box up the rattles and spoons and send them to less fortunate children. Since I didn't have a baby and therefore had more time on my hands, I volunteered to FedEx the items for her. So she was painlessly unburdened of some of her plenteousness, and when I discounted the rattles and spoons from the prices in the turquoise catalogue they sold on eBay like hotcakes.

I've been sending Ma a check on a regular basis, so she's able to continue with her self-improvement. Once the leaking's under control, she'll get an operation to fix the loose flaps of skin on the back of her arms and another to rid her skin of flaws. Plus with this renewed optimism I have trebled my willpower and am able to fit into the repaired yak pants and even the most challenging of the blusas. Soon, with Penelope's help, Mike and I will finish the paperwork and get our own infant from overseas. Over me pours the calorieless vanilla calm of gratitude.

Again

Jim and Mary Ford had done it all wrong. Now they were talking about a divorce.

"It was the 60s. No one could raise a kid right. The drugs, the disorder," Carol said. She was their only daughter, with her tattooed arms. She had brought hijiki salad for brunch. It didn't really go with the brioche.

"It looks like wet twigs," Jim said.

"Wait till you taste it," said Mary.

On top of everything else (vegan, broke), Carol wasn't married. She'd experimented with sex, drugs, communal living. From her diet and not enough uninterrupted sleep she was skinny as a stalk, with bags under her eyes and the pallor of a parsnip. She had chained herself to luxury cars owned by bigwig politicians, had been dragged out of conventions for tearing open her blouse to reveal oppositional slogans written on her body. Her teeth had never been fixed. She lived in Berkeley and made asymmetrical mobiles for a living. There was always some hard-luck case sleeping on her floor.

How Jim Ford's dutiful sperm, working their way up toward the egg that for all Mary's interest in sex might well have been waiting for the onslaught in a terrycloth robe with a copy of *Ladies' Home Journal* and a glass of Nestea, produced the offspring that was their Carol was the great mystery of Mary and Jim's lives. They loved their daughter, with her dent between the eyebrows just like Jim's when she was thinking hard and her deft, pudgy hands that were replicas of Mary's. Yet they didn't know what to make of her, this person they'd cooked up after a few bourbon-and-Cokes in a room at the Kew Motor Inn on their wedding night. 1966: Mary, virginal and ignorant, her hair lacquered as a piece of furniture. When Jim climbed on top of her, her only thought had been not to cry; it would smear her eyes and make her look like a rodent.

"Look," Carol said. She couldn't stand the thought of her parents apart. "We could try again."

"You'd do that?"

"For us?"

᠍

She took off her shoes. She took off the hemp jumper she was wearing, all her jewelry (she made asymmetrical mobile earrings as well), barrettes she'd been wearing since she decided to grow out her hair.

Her mother sat on the bed and put the bag of Jordan almonds she was eating from on the nightstand. "Jim," she said, "you're going to have to help her."

"I'm helping! See? I'm helping!" Jim Ford rolled up his sleeves.

There was a photo of Carol and her high-school prom date on her mother's dresser. No one had wanted to go with Carol Ford, all hairy legs and feminist attitude, so she had asked a junior, who'd gone out of pity or a desire to hang out with seniors. He'd worn a short red jacket that made him look like a maître d'. Worse, he was taking painkillers for tennis elbow and had rebuffed her advances on the way home in the limo. Some prom date, she'd complained to her mother. "I mean, if you can't lose your virginity at the *prom* . . . !"

In her mother's jewelry box was the charm bracelet Carol had once been caught working on with a pair of tweezers. There had been a little gold cage with a bill folded smaller than a thumbnail wedged inside it. When she got it out it was only a dollar, barely enough for Twizzlers and a Coke. For messing with other people's property Carol had been required to endure the longest lecture in history. Her father had added a sidebar about the folly of greed. There were quotes from Shakespeare and Ben Franklin, from Gandhi or the Dalai freaking Lama.

"And if it was a hundred what would you have done with it, young lady?"

"I would've sent it to Mrs. Qwee," she'd said. "Her family doesn't even have *shoes*." Never mind that Mrs. Qwee, who had lived with the Fords for a year in the late 70s, was back in Vietnam by then. She was the only person Carol had been able to think of who didn't own anything.

Sometimes she'd wished her parents would just smack her and be done with it.

She took off her socks.

Now, as she stood in her bra and underwear, Jim Ford averted his eyes. His daughter hadn't been naked in front of him since she was a little kid.

Her mother reached for the remote and turned off the TV. "Lord in heaven, let's just get through this."

Fortunately, Carol was a small woman and her mother was large. Her head fit adequately (hadn't she once heard people were born with a head the size it'd be for life?), and her father's callused hands gave her feet a final push.

It took time for her eyes to adjust. Fluid seeped into her nose, down her throat. She thought of astronauts. In eighth grade there had been a trip to the Smithsonian, where she'd gotten freeze dried ice cream like they ate in space. Longings beset her immediately: for a foil packet of dry ice cream, a beach read, her mother.

Two things she hadn't counted on: the monotony and the loneliness. The first time around she'd been a brain stem, blank as celery. Now she had memories. Her day planner sat where she'd left it on the kitchen counter. She hated those anal-retentive Franklin Covey ones with all the pockets and inserts, but one of the women at the nursing home where Carol taught art had given it to her as a Christmas gift.

Before that she had really struggled to keep appointments straight. Now, taking nutrients through her umbilical cord, she didn't have to find time for grocery shopping or making meals. She had never learned to like cooking, in spite of her father's rah-rahs about one-pot meals—hadn't he even bought her a Crock-Pot cookbook at some point?

All this time had opened up in her schedule, and she couldn't get anything done.

One thing she'd never been good at was telling jokes. There was one about the pope and a guy named Bubba that she loved, but she always forgot the middle part. At how many dinner parties had she disappointed herself by starting that joke and then flubbing it three-quarters of the way through? It was maddening. At one time she'd also known by heart the prologue to *Romeo and Juliet* and a poem called "The Sun Rising." In college her poetry teacher had come into class one day with a bandage wrapped around his head. Car accident? He was always getting into car accidents.

"What's this poem about?"

No one said anything. The bandage was distracting. Carol had some guesses. "Carol, get us started."

"Busy old fool, unruly sun, / Why dost thou thus, / Through windows, and through curtains call on us? / Must to thy motions lovers' seasons run?" She went along like this for a bit. "Saucy pedantic wretch, go chide / Late school boys and sour prentices . . ." She had no idea what the fuck she was talking about. Even memorizing the poem hadn't made it make sense. Now here she was, dying to remember what came after sour prentices, and she didn't have a pen to write it down (that had helped her recall in the past) or enough light to see. And on top of that, her lovely hands were retreating into nubs.

Yet the monotony of gestation was not uninterrupted. At regular intervals, music played. A favorite was Mozart, though sprinkled in were *Peer Gynt* and jazz interpretations of "My Favorite Things." Off-limits, it seemed, were Woody Guthrie, Pete Seeger, Jimi Hendrix, the protest songs that had been the soundtrack to Jim and Mary's lives the first time around. For a while Carol was able to remember the words to "Woodstock" (it was the Joni Mitchell version she heard), but after a time that began to fade. What of the life she had lived? What of the person she had been?

She heard her father's voice and the pounding of nails in wood. He was back in his workshop. A good sign. His deep baritone resonated; he was coming in close.

Sometimes swaying movements accompanied the music. Where in the split ranch were they dancing? Down the front hallway? In the living room, now crowded with thirty years of knickknacks and souvenirs? There had never been much room. For a time she thought of having legs that extended and walked the earth. Legs, those first vehicles to carry us away from our parents. We crawl and walk, and then one day we're on a bus to New York.

⁂

Early in the second trimester the hiccups began.

How had Mary forgotten that? Her mother and sister, too, had suffered pregnancy hiccups. She tried holding her breath, sipping from a glass of water while pinching her nose and ears shut, saying "grapefruit" over and over again, until she remembered that was supposed to prevent not hiccups but sneezing.

She was tired all the time. After all, she wasn't twenty-two anymore. In thirty years she had gained weight and lost the muscle tone she'd had when she was a dance minor in college. Now she had varicose veins, acid reflux, vaginal dryness. For her fiftieth birthday a friend had given her a certificate for racquetball lessons. She had ripped her Achilles tendon her first day out. On top of that her cholesterol was high. She hardly ever slept through the night. Sometimes she woke with a start, her head bathed in sweat. How had she failed to notice? She was perimenopausal, for Christ's sake.

Propped against two pillows, Jim was folding down pages in *Beyond Jennifer and Jason*. His current issue of *Machine Design* sat on the bedside table. He had moved his stuff back up from the guest room.

"What about Helga?"

"Helga?"

"Helga sounds like someone capable. Proud Norsewoman. I see her holding an axe."

"I'm not naming anything that comes out of me Helga." She ran her hand over her belly. It was going to be a big baby.

"What about Carol again? We liked Carol the first time around."

Jim flipped through to a page he'd earmarked. "Sierra? Miriam? Maybe Martha. That's a name you can grow into."

"Carol hated that name."

"She did? I never knew that."

They fell quiet. It hadn't occurred to them until this moment that in electing for Carol to be born again, they would lose their original Carol. Despite all her flaws, her dietary restrictions and odd tattoos (PEACH LOVE ALL, one said. The tattoo artist had sort of messed up the E), Mary and Jim had loved their daughter. She'd had a great sense of humor. She'd been able to recite—

"What was it she liked to recite, Jim?"

"Oh, boy. That kid knew a lot of things. That poem about suffering. I think she knew *Romeo and Juliet* pretty much by heart."

"The whole thing?"

Jim considered. "Well, maybe not all of it. But she had the gist. I remember one time I took her to see *La Cage aux Folles*." She was reciting lines on the way home on the train. The passengers loved it."

"She was never very good at jokes."

"You would think she would be. It's not much different from lines in a play."

"I think she got performance anxiety. She was so worried no one would laugh."

"But *she* was a great laugher."

"And then she would start laughing while she was telling the joke. Thinking ahead to the punch line."

"That drove people crazy. She would be laughing so hard she wouldn't be able to finish it."

"I remember." Mary said. A whole raft of memories was coming back. "Remember that tofurkey?"

"The who?"

"She brought one on Thanksgiving. Everything was made out of tofu. It even had little molded drumsticks."

"I think that was the same Thanksgiving she brought those Chinese exchange students and the family from Darfur with their little nuts and seeds, or whatever they were."

"Jim, don't exaggerate."

"I'm just saying, that crossed my mind when she volunteered." He pointed to his wife's midsection. "You can't save everyone. Especially when you're doing arts and crafts instead of making a living."

"She had a job in retail."

"Retail schmetail."

More and more now she slept. She dreamt of floating and flying, colorful kaleidoscopic blurs and whirls that brought back days of popping a tab of LSD or eating mushrooms with the poetry teacher.

"Chokecherry, chokecherry," he said. It was, he claimed, the single most poetic word in English. He called the house where he lived The Homestead. It had a composting toilet. Carol had pedaled over there on Friday morning, when his wife was at work. That was nearly half her life ago; she hadn't thought about Old Chokecherry in years. She had lost her virginity to that man, with his John Lennon glasses and his unwashed boxers, his prodigious memory for poems. He would recite Whitman in bed, Yeats, Roethke. *The shapes a bright container can contain.* What a mind-blower for an eighteen-year-old. Admittedly, she'd set the bar pretty low back at the prom with the maître d'. It was as she was thinking about the poetry teacher and the great things he'd taught her that she realized she was awake and rocking. The fluid was sloshing as if she were inside a jar of water being rolled around on the floor.

It came to her. The photos her father had taken of her mother when she was pregnant the first time. Hundreds of them. Mary on the steps of the Lincoln Memorial. In front of the Washington Monument. The Capitol. A Chinese restaurant. The public library. The kitchen. The bathtub. Which is all to say, Jim became enchanted with Mary when she was pregnant. Never in her life had he taken so many photos of her as he had then. She was radiant, irresistible.

What must it be like, after thirty years, for him to see his wife pregnant again?

A baritone moan. Then a higher-pitched one.

Carol tried to distract herself. One never wants to be present at the primal scene, even in utero. A deck of cards would have been useful. "From forth the fatal loins of these two foes / a pair of star-cross'd lovers take their life," she recited in her head. Life, or lives?

"Whose misadventured piteous overthrows / do with their death bury their parents' strife." She wished she had memorized more things.

In college, Carol became known as one of the Cherries. It started when she took Critical Reading freshman year. He'd come to that class with a bandaged head, too. Was he still alive now? How was his head? She had never been good at mental math. Now, when she was born again, he would be sixty-eight years her senior. It made the twenty-five years between them when they'd first met seem paltry. By the time she'd be old enough to have another affair with him, he'd be, at minimum, eighty-five. No teeth. He'd probably be catheterized, and demented from being conked in the head with garden implements by his angry wife. That made Carol want to contact him. He could go get himself born again, too. But of course his mother would almost certainly be dead. And you couldn't go climbing up into just anyone.

Sometimes through the membranes and fluid came cooing, an animal language that soothed her. When she was born again, would Carol still be Carol? She had always liked her name. For a time she mourned this loss, wondering who she would be next.

Hopefully not a Martha. What sort of parenting strategies would Mary and Jim use? Last time around, it had been Dr. Spock and some vague existential notions Jim picked up in a philosophy elective. Carol had been raised without a creed, without belief in Jesus or Buddha or even a beneficent Earth. Though she had sometimes regretted not having religion, she dreaded the thought of her mother dressing her up in a pinafore and hauling her off to Sunday school.

&

Both of them were sleeping poorly. Mary was in her last trimester and had the hiccups more often, it seemed, than she didn't have them. Jim couldn't get it out of his mind that he had been close to giving Carol the one name she hated. What else didn't he know about his daughter? Maybe all those years she had only pretended to enjoy going to the Javits Center with him to see the boat show. Or those thousand-piece puzzles he'd given her for her birthday each year. What if she'd hated sitting with him at his drafting table those Sunday afternoons, putting together Escher staircases and the ceiling of the Sistine Chapel?

It wasn't a restful night for Carol, either. She'd begun thinking about all the things she'd have to do over again. Adolescence. Kindergarten. Toilet training. She'd been too freaked out by tampons the first time she got her period and had to go to school wearing a maxi pad that felt like she was holding a roll of paper towels between her thighs. In Home Ec, Elisa Pileggi had congratulated her. Out loud. In front of everyone. Carol had thought she must be bleeding through her jeans. She only found out later that her own mother had talked to Elisa's mother on the phone the night before.

The thought of having to go through all that again was almost un-bearable. If she could do it with the benefit of her adult insight and understanding, she might be able to stand it. If only she'd taken a cell phone in with her. She could've called and told them the deal was off, it was a stupid idea in the first place, get an abortion. She didn't want to be a different person; she just wanted to be plain old Carol again, with her misspelled tattoo and her mobiles. She missed her studio, her subscriptions to underground zines, her mobiles twisting and glinting in the afternoon light.

&

"The colic," Jim said.
Mary nodded. "The sleepless nights."

"Remember how bad your postpartum was? That was before they really even knew about that kind of depression."

"And oh God, the separation anxiety. I could barely get her on the school bus."

"She had those terrible allergies. Remember how bad her asthma was? I tried everything. I put her in the tub with garlic."

"Where did you get that cockamamie idea?"

"Some magazine. The only thing that worked when she got bad like that was adrenaline shots."

"Then she puked her guts out."

"But after that she could breathe for days. She could race me down the block."

The phone rang again. In the past couple months there had been a lot of calls.

"She hasn't shown up for her shift at the ASPCA auction," a woman said. "She gave this number as an alternate."

"She's sort of in limbo right now."

Carol had signed up to walk or swim or bike all sorts of-thons. There were dogs and kittens she had promised to foster, diseases she had pledged her asymmetrical mobiles to raise money to cure. There were calls from NARAL and the ACLU, the Sierra Club and Greenpeace, Planned Parenthood and PETA, CARE and DARE.

One morning, Jim opened the door to a man in a plaid tam who handed him a leash. At the other end of it was a three-legged pug.

"Name of Andy. You'd be surprised at how well this little critter can get around."

Three women, two of them in wheelchairs, came to call. Jim and the third, who managed pretty well for herself on a cane, maneuvered the wheelchairs as far as the porch.

"It's a split ranch," he apologized.

"Carol built a *ramp*," said the one on the cane.

"That's a very special daughter you've got there, Mr. Ford. When did you say she'll be back from that meditation retreat?"

"Art therapy's made all the difference in the world to us."

Jim called the Assist-a-Bus to take them back into town. "No wonder she never got around to getting a real job," he told Mary.

"The boat people had a big effect on her. Carol kept asking where Mrs. Qwee's suitcase was, and I kept trying to explain she didn't *have* a suitcase."

"Christ, she didn't even have teeth."

"A few teeth."

"Yeah, and then someone at school told her the gooks had pulled out Mrs. Qwee's teeth. Remember that? She had nightmares for weeks."

"That was I think what got her started with her whole Holocaust fascination." Mary lowered herself into a chair. She needed to get off her feet for a while. "She was always a sensitive child. From the time she was a baby she would startle. It didn't even have to be a particularly loud noise."

"The boat people must have been hard for her to fathom. All of a sudden here's this ancient little toothless woman who didn't speak a word of English living with us."

"Remember how Carol was trying to get us all to learn sign language?"

"I think she and Mrs. Qwee actually learned a little."

The homeless HIV-positive teenage girls were noisy and left their Popsicle sticks on the porch stairs. For sick people they had huge appetites.

"This ranch dip is great," one said. "Though Carol's always saying we should stay away from dairy. Weakens the immune system."

"Carol's really great," the one with bangs said. She had a peaches-and-cream complexion and auburn hair not unlike Carol's. "I wish I'd had a mother like Carol. My mother's a total crackhead. She's never even seen any of the pottery I made."

"Pottery?"

"We're making bowls for refugees. Next she was going to show us how to do tureens. Where did you say she went?"

Mary showed the girls the linen closet, and they made up the guestroom beds. It was difficult now for her to negotiate the stairs to the landing of the split ranch. Her back ached constantly; she always had to pee.

The HIV-positive girls surrendered their beds and moved to the sofas when the amputee veterans arrived.

✍

Increasingly, she wanted only to practice sucking or grasping. Her mind was blank for long stretches, then full briefly and scrambled like eggs. *Thy seasons' motions love must run.* The desire for vodka fell away, the desire for personal betterment. Ditto old Chokecherry and the rest of his gender. A yen for oysters gave way to noodles, strained peas, mashed bananas, milk. Syntax fell away, and grammar. Finally words themselves and the sympathies they contained. All went with a wet pop as a baby shot nameless and screaming into the world.

On the Fords' doorstep, most of a Sudanese village stood patiently, wooden bowls in their hands.

Outlandish Plot

The plot: an American woman and an Irishman are having a thing. A what? A thing. He's married—that makes it a thing. If he weren't married, it might be a romance; it might be the most fulfilling blah-blah either of them has ever known. As it is, with a marriage in the middle of it, a thing. How did they meet? Over a tray of bread. It wasn't wine and roses. It started just up the road from the Fink Bread Company in Long Island City, across the river from Manhattan. He drives a bread truck; she works at the vitamin store on the corner. When he makes deliveries to the deli near the vitamin store, he collects stale dinner rolls, squished jelly donuts, misshapen Danishes oozing their cheese, the daily damaged cache of carbohydrates. Stale for fresh, stale for fresh, and over time, over the bread tray, over the abbreviated exchange of sidewalk niceties and coffee-getting, over his hangovers and hers, over the everyday patter that showcases his Irish brogue and her good American teeth, something blooms between them. What blooms? A thing.

The American woman wants to be a writer. The Irishman wants not to be married. She—Evie Myerson, her name is—is trying to write a novel about an Irishman and an American woman. She's hoping it's not just a thing they're having. One complication: the Irishman keeps waffling on the issue of his marriage. There's a separation, a getting back together, another separation, another getting back together.

Evie Myerson would rather not be selling vitamins at a health-food store in Long Island City and having a thing with a married man. She would rather, for instance, be signing copies of her novel at the Barnes & Noble in Soho and living in swank digs. It appears that book signings in Soho and cohabiting swankly with the Irishman are about as likely to come to pass within the next quarter century as is the election of a lesbian president of the United States. Evie doesn't deny this. She's a realist. What surprises her is that none of these events seems possible even in her fiction. The part about working at a vitamin store seems to insist on being imported straight from the life into the book, though Evie would like to make the female character a stuntwoman, an emergency medical technician, a college admissions officer. Someone with skills.

Skills, okay. Skills were fine, but maybe Evie Myerson wouldn't have to handle situations involving teenagers or blood. Maybe a career change wouldn't even be necessary. How about a change of scenery? It could still be a vitamin store, but not a struggling one in Long Island City, Manhattan's glamourless, warehouse-pimpled stepsister. The vitamin store could be transplanted to Vail, where people can afford a forty-dollar bottle of antioxidants. Or Missoula, a place she has always thought she'd like to live. Though how to get an Irish immigrant to Missoula?

This is a Tuesday morning, delivery day at the vitamin store. Evie checks in the order and gets to opening boxes. How many days since her last period? Pregnancy isn't part of the plot of her novel, but fifteen minutes in the back of the Fink Bread truck with Brendan Fahey was, about two weeks ago, a development in the plot of her life.

Brendan Fahey is amiable and overworked. He has no lower back teeth on either side; he drinks his paychecks, cries at movies, curses in Irish, worships Pierce Brosnan, tells Evie she's a madwoman and a whore all together. She understands this to be a compliment. He likes to eat with his hands. He likes to pick up the fried eggs and lay them on the toast and nosedive the egg-and-toast into a pool of ketchup. He delivers for the Fink Bread Company during the day and, some nights, bartends at McReilly's on Vernon Boulevard, just down the road from the vitamin store. They both work here, Evie and Brendan, in Long Island City, real estate's booby prize for overshooting the suburbs, for falling just short of Manhattan.

It's been thirty-seven days since her last period.

A baby, an abortion: neither is supposed to be part of the plot.

The plot: a plane crashes into the World Trade Center. The radio next to the cash register is saying a plane went off course and crashed. Evie is heading to the bathroom in the back of the store. Big mishaps are always being reported in Manhattan. Trains run late and people are pushed in front of them. On those days, trains run later. It might be a cramp she feels in her gut. It might be. Then the plot would be stopped in its tracks: no abortion, no baby, no regrets she didn't hurry to a clinic for a morning-after pill after the tryst in the back of the Fink Bread truck with Brendan Fahey.

In the bathroom, she peers at the face in the shard of mirror over the sink. The face is decorated with gray eyeliner and dabs of flesh-colored concealer under each eye. The concealer's not rubbed in properly. Is this the face of a woman harboring an Irish-American zygote? She's twenty-six years old, has no savings, lives in an apartment approximately the size of a sport utility vehicle two blocks from the Midtown Tunnel. She owns a laptop, two futile novel starts, an unmade bed, a six-pack of Tequiza. This last not because she likes agave-flavored beer, but because Brendan Fahey likes agave-flavored beer and she likes Brendan Fahey.

A plane crashed into the World Trade Center. Was that what she heard?

Why did she have unprotected sex with Brendan Fahey in the back of a bread truck? Because. Because they don't need to sneak around like that anymore; because Brendan Fahey's divorce will go through some-time next month. He says. Because the instant you don't have to sneak around anymore is the very instant having unprotected sex in the back of a bread truck starts to sound like a good idea. In the novel Evie's try-ing to write, the Irishman and the American woman are talking about moving to Missoula. They'll start saving money, they'll buy secondhand hiking boots. They'll use condoms always. They're going to have sex at night, horizontally, in the bed, with condoms, spermicidal jelly, etcetera, etcetera. Whereas the real Evie Myerson has a scrape on her hip from a latch on the bread truck.

There's a commotion on the sidewalk. The Italians from the deli next door are outside, everyone with their backs to the vitamin store's plate-glass window. Arms are flailing. Someone in a white coat and houndstooth chef's pants is kneeling on the sidewalk. Why is that person kneeling? Maybe someone has been hit by a car. Evie steps outside. In the distance, smoke. Everyone out here is saying the same sentence, some with the inflections wrong, like members of a foreign-language class learning to greet each other in the new tongue. And, ridiculously, as if the repeated words are conjuring the event, a plume of fire-laced smoke blanks out the tops of the towers.

Someone has brought out a radio. It's not just the newscaster repeating the plot; the plot is repeating the plot. A plane crashes into the World Trade Center; a plane crashes into the World Trade Center. Two towers, two planes. Events double, a terrible doppelgangering that is also a splitting in half. A big knife has sliced down into history; now history is two halves and everything before this moment is one part and everything after this moment is another part and they can't be slapped back together, any more than a head severed from a neck can be slapped back on to make the body a person again. Terrorists have hijacked commercial jets and crashed them into the World Trade Center. Everyone standing on the sidewalk hears that explanation. Then everyone rewinds the scene and moves the buildings off to the right. To the left, to the right: Evie tilts the Twin Towers forty-five degrees, just for a moment, until the planes pass. Then pushes them upright again. See how easy? The plot is a bad plot; it's clumsy and stupid. It needs better writers; it needs an editor.

People wander into the vitamin store and drink water and leave. People nibble on PowerBars and Balance Bars. What empty promises, this balance, this power!

Armageddon's delivering a portable hell to Manhattan, but, thankfully, Brendan Fahey's in Flushing. Evie holds on to that through midmorning, through noon and the hours that come after. There's no phone call from him, but he doesn't deliver in Manhattan. She distributes bottles of water to people on the sidewalk. The guys from the deli offer cans of beer, and everyone stands and sips and weeps and watches the portable hell hover over Lower Manhattan.

Outside are noise and bad sights and smells, but inside is worse. Inside, in the bathroom, there is still the reflection of a face, though now the eyes are blurry with tears and truly terrified. Something primal and tiny might be happening inside the body below that face. Something might be happening inside the borders of Evie. But out there, inside the borders of Manhattan, something primal and gigantic is happening for certain.

෯

"Box cutters," Brendan says. "I can't believe they did it with box cutters." Two days have passed; it's time for stiff drinks. In this case, a succession of Tequizas, like a royal family, though royalty is one of Brendan Fahey's least favorite things. Still, he's doing better than Evie is. He's more used to terror, having grown up in Belfast on a steady diet of bombs and martyrs.

On TV, they're saying no more steak knives on planes.

Also, no more aerosol hairspray, corkscrews, nail clippers, scissors, wire hangers, glass bottles, tweezers, pocketknives, letter openers, box cutters.

"Feckin' box cutters," Brendan says again. For years he has used box cutters daily, never imagining them to be instruments of terror. To him, they're instruments of cardboard-cutting. It amazes him to think of them this way, as much as it would amaze him to think of his hands as instruments of terror. He keeps an X-Acto knife in the right front pocket of his work shirt, just below the cursive "Brendan" sewed in red thread. He keeps taking out the knife and turning it over in his hands.

There's no good way to say this next thing.

"I know this is—ah—bad timing, but I think I might be pregnant." There. She has said it. Two Tequizas in, she's said it. It seems a small and homely thing now, this maybe of a pregnancy, this possible pin drop amid topple and ruin.

"You're not pregnant."

"How do you know?"

"You're having a panic attack. You're panicking. Calm yourself and you'll get your period." As he's saying this, Brendan is looking half at her, half at the towers toppling on TV. First it was his wife who divided his attention; now anyone who wants it has to squeeze in between two toppling towers.

"I'm serious, Brendan. I'm not panicking. I was thinking this before all that happened."

This is how they have learned to speak, these last forty-eight hours. *I thought that before this. I was thinking this before that.* As if this thing, this new portable hell (who even knew hell was portable?) that installed itself in Manhattan, with satellite hells in Washington and the Pennsylvania woods, has absconded with all the good nouns.

Wedding. Promotion. Pregnancy. Future. Even if you did want to use those words now, they don't mean what they used to. But neither do the new words. They aren't accurate, either. *Before the bombing.* That's what people are saying. Technically, though, it wasn't a bomb. A bomb is a bowling ball with a fuse. A bomb is what goes off in the Tom and Jerry cartoons and somehow—temporarily, always temporarily!—shears the fur off the cat. A plane with seventy people in it, a plane with moms and dads and uncles and sons and a scout for a professional basketball team called the Wizards (who even knew there was a professional basketball team called the Wizards?) and a right-wingish CNN commentator who was annoying, all right, but never annoying enough to wish death on; a plane containing thirty-three or so microwaved teriyaki beef meals in white plastic trays and thirty-three or so Asian chicken meals, a plane containing multiple partial sets of American Tourister luggage and clean underwear folded and dirty underwear stuffed in plastic bags and souvenirs for the kids (snow globes, keychains, T-shirts of the "My Parents Went to Boston and All I Got Was This Lousy T-Shirt" variety), and 106 copies of the in-flight magazine with cover article about Christopher Reeve's post-accident travels in a wheelchair, and 150 unused barf bags—that was not a bomb. That was a big slice of life transporting itself from one part of America to another, because Americans are always in motion and being in motion is one of the main things about being an American.

"I'm not panicking. I'm being realistic." Evie the realist. She's a realist like John Steinbeck was a realist, with his dusty Joads heading west and his hungry lamb feeding from the breast of a woman or his hungry infant feeding from the breast of a lamb. Which was it? In high school, other girls wrote their book reports on *A Tree Grows in Brooklyn*. Not Evie. Steinbeck knocked her out. Even Zola and the rest of the Naturalists knocked her out, with their depressing French villages and their deadly mine shafts. People did die in mine shafts; people starved to death every day of the week.

The plot: nineteen Arab men come to the United States and learn how to fly so they can hijack commercial airplanes and carry out simultaneous suicide missions aimed at symbolic American targets that also happen to be office buildings filled with people. How is all this going to be accomplished? With will. Will and box cutters.

Once, when Evie took a class at Gotham Writers' Workshop, the students told her it wasn't plausible for the female character in her story to fall in love with a woman and just hightail it out of a twenty-year marriage. *It's not motivated*, the teacher said. Oh, it's motivated all right, Evie thought, picturing her mother and the new girlfriend. It's not believable, members of the class said, and Evie, naïve Evie, went home crying because of course it wasn't believable—she couldn't believe it, either! That fiction teacher would have sat those terrorists down and told them a thing or two. She would have told them their plot wasn't motivated. She would have told them it wasn't believable.

Brendan gets another beer out of the refrigerator. "This is the last Tequiza," he says.

The Last Tequiza: A Novel. Evie's always looking for titles, but this one's a little portentous, a little too *Dances with Wolves*.

"If you get the last Tequiza, what do I get?" Drunk is what she wants to get, but Brendan's had four to her two.

How about a kiss from the person with the last Tequiza? They're on her unmade bed, kissing, their hands under each other's shirts. "We can't get drunk and fool around," she says.

Brendan sits up. He has a tattoo of interlocking Celtic patterns ringed around his upper arm. Evie loves that tattoo. For the first time she thinks she would like to kiss it. She should kiss it right now, because who knows? Tomorrow, Brendan Fahey and his Celtic arm might get blown to smithereens. Tonight, all over Manhattan and its boroughs and the towns and villages beyond, new widows are thinking about the arms of their beloveds, blown to smithereens. If only Smithereens were a town in Ireland, with an eighteen-hole golf course and twelve pubs. You could be blown to Smithereens and back again, after a round of golf and a few pints.

"For feck's sake," Brendan says. "We always get drunk and fool around."

"That was before this."

They sit in silence for a moment, the only sounds the whine of sirens in the distance. The Twin Towers are gone. If you live in Long Island City, you live always and forever in the shadow of Manhattan's showoff of a skyline. Now no more World Trade Center on that skyline. It was like turning toward your husband in bed to wish him good morning and discovering his eyes were gone. Could the two of you, forty-eight hours later, he eyeless as a mushroom, get drunk and make love? Of course you couldn't. But what else could you do? Go looking for his eyes?

"Brendan?" Evie's crying now. She's a broke wannabe writer, possibly pregnant by a married Irishman with whom she's having a thing, and now this badly located apartment—badly located because it's in the industrial suburbs of Queens, badly located because it's two blocks from the Midtown Tunnel—suddenly seems unimaginably badder. Is *badder* a word? It is now. If an American Airlines plane can be a bomb, *badder* can be a word. Now she lives not just in a warehouse district near the Midtown Tunnel, but a hop, skip, and a jump from the site of the worst terrorist attack ever, and maybe not far at all from what could be, in the future, the new worst-terrorist-attack-ever site, for who knows what they might come up with tomorrow?

"Brendan?" Crying harder now, and grabbing for his arm. Not that arm, the other one—the one with the tattoo. Now trying to kiss that arm, but aiming wrong and getting his elbow in her face. She tries to feel for the tattoo against her forehead. Shouldn't the tattooed skin feel different? Shouldn't there be a Celtic Braille for her lips to read?

"What are you after, Evie?" Brendan asks, and pulls her to him, so that instead of a kiss on his tattoo, all she leaves there is a slobbery sob and nose goo.

"I want to move to Missoula."

"Oh, my Evie."

Something swerves in her innards. Maybe it's Brendan Fahey's unprecedented use of the possessive pronoun. She shivers in his arms, the tattooed one and the other one, her whole body vibrating like a tuning fork, and then he gets up off the bed and heads back to Flushing, where he still shares an apartment with his wife, and when she goes to the bathroom before bed she finds it's not Brendan Fahey's unprecedented use of the possessive pronoun that's swerving her innards. It's just her uterine lining sloughing off its monthly cells.

Cells. She pictures a tiny terrorist inside each one.

Here they are in Missoula. Look at these trees and wide open spaces, smell that fresh mountain air, look at that truck driver with an umbrella in his gun rack and those other truck drivers with guns in their gun racks. Witness the health-food store with a macrobiotic deli patronized by women wearing Birkenstocks with socks! There must be a farmhouse to buy here, so that when the baby is born, the baby and the sheepdog can flourish and grow sturdy in verdant pastures. Aren't verdant pastures where children and pets are sent to grow sturdy?

It won't work. It has to. She can't set the novel in New York: Terrorists have torn up her setting. As if New York wasn't a daunting enough setting for a novel already. But now, after *this*, novels set in New York will have to be set in the New York with Twin Towers or the New York without them. If neither of those options avails, Missoula. But how to get an Irish immigrant to Missoula? People emigrating from Ireland don't buy plane tickets to Montana. They buy plane tickets to New York or Boston and get jobs at Irish bars and live in New York or Boston for years before moving a few miles out to the suburbs. Maybe some blaze a trail to the heart of the country, but not the Brendan Faheys, who live for the Gaelic football beamed live by satellite to pubs in Queens.

There. Her two hours of writing are up. She has conjured an outlandish fantasy about an Irishman and an American woman and their baby moving to a farm in Missoula. It's neither motivated nor believable; nineteen terrorists hijacking four commercial jets and slamming them into the Twin Towers (both!) and also the Pentagon, let's not forget by the way the Pentagon, is more plausible than this farm in Missoula, with the sheepdog and the verdant pastures. Now it's 8:45 a.m., time to troop down the street to the vitamin store and sell vitamins. It should come as no surprise to anyone that vitamin stores haven't exactly been doing a brisk business since the attacks. The air, after all, is filled with fine particulate pollution; specifically, 220 floors of vaporized people and office memos. And the air is filled with talk of what those terrorists are cooking up next: anthrax attacks? a smallpox epidemic? But sure, honey, I'll stop in at the vitamin store on the way home from work and pick up some B-complex.

It's Tuesday again: one week since the attacks. A delivery will come this morning, but there won't be many boxes to open. The only products moving are sleep aids and nerve calmers: valerian, melatonin, anything with chamomile. Also Rescue Remedy, promising to be "effective in virtually any situation that causes stress or anxiety." She's reading off the label now, to a customer with a baby swaddled to her chest and concealer dabbed hastily under each eye. "Helps restore a sense of calm and control." Calm—ha! Control—ha! But Americans are buying it. This customer with her baby swaddled to her is buying it. For all that America's faith in its unbreachable borders has been breached, the belief that calm and control can be bought in a bottle has not.

"Will that be all for you today?" Evie has the Rescue Remedy the woman has decided on ($15.95), but the woman has paused near the herbal teas. Browsing again, with the shopper's acquisitive eye. Maybe things have started to return to normal. Things, it's true, may never return to normal, but in the world of retail sales, returning to normal just means getting back in the swing of the old pre-terrorist buying patterns.

Consumers better get back to it, or Evie Myerson and umpteen other people are out of a job.

There's a tap on Evie's back. "Take the baby."

A baby is being handed to her. It's the only calm face Evie has seen in days. "This is a nice baby," she says. Like a consumer she says it.

"Take the baby. Please take him. He's a good baby."

"Is he your baby?" Like a consumer buying something on the street that might have fallen off the truck. A Rolex watch, a Prada bag. A baby.

"He's my baby," the woman says.

I don't mean maybe. The song comes storming wildly through Evie's head. Do panic attacks come with soundtracks?

"My husband. I haven't seen my husband since the planes." The woman is rocking a little now, back and forth on her heels. Evie notices how she didn't notice the woman's disheveled hair and clothing, though right away she'd noticed the concealer.

"I can take care of this baby for you for a few hours. But I can't take this baby. It's your baby." Evie's babbling now, her eyes brimming with tears, her nose filling with goo. This isn't how it works. This isn't the mother-baby economy. The mother can't just give the baby away, any more than the mother can put the baby up for sale on eBay.

The mother is edging toward the door, the way someone trapped in a bad conversation at a cocktail party edges toward the door.

"No. No way." Evie, naïve Evie, with her bad job and her bad apartment and her bad novel and her period—she's not up for playing the fairy godmother. "Take your baby back," she says, another misplaced pop lyric. There should be doo-wopping. There should be backup. Yes. There should be backup.

"Please," the woman says. Then she's out the door.

Oh, no you don't. Evie, dashing toward the door, almost says it, like a character in a cops-and-robbers movie. *Get back here, you dastardly baby-leaver.* In real life, she can only shout "Hey!" and "Stop!" as she hurries after the woman down Vernon Boulevard. But she's carrying a baby and a bottle of Rescue Remedy, and she's wearing clogs, and the woman has a sprinter's stride. The woman must be heading to the Vernon-Jackson subway station. Evie will follow her there—a train never comes when you need it—and before the doors close, she'll give this baby back. "You want your baby back," she'll say to the woman, more pop lyrics, and the woman will want her baby back, and this unwieldy plot will be shrunk down to an anecdote.

She catches her clog heel on the curb and, for a bad second, loses her footing.

She has to stop. One thing worse than being the stranger to whom someone gives a baby is being the stranger brought to court for dropping and thus maiming or killing said baby. She fits the clog back on her foot and keeps after the woman, though at a slower pace, and she sees the woman descend the station's Manhattan-bound stairs. "Don't leave me," she says under her breath, and stops herself from adding "this way."

The baby is starting to cry now, the kind of cry that's a gearing-up to a bawl. "Don't worry—we'll get her," Evie tells the baby. She and the baby are buddy cops now, pursuing a fugitive.

The subway doors are closing with a pneumatic hiss as she reaches the bottom of the stairs. "Stop that train!" she hears herself shout, like any other New York crazy person.

With a description and a few other details (sprinter, Manhattan-bound, husband dead in World Trade Center), the NYPD should be able to reunite this baby with his mother, Evie tells herself as she heads back to the store. If not NYPD, then FBI. If they can identify a person killed in the World Trade Center with nothing more to go on than a few hairs or a toothbrush, finding that mother will be a walk in the park.

Back at the store, nothing seems to be amiss, though one customer has left cash payment on the counter beside a handwritten note listing the items purchased. Who would have imagined such a small-town gesture, here in the big city? Then again, who would have imagined anyone around here handing off a baby to a stranger?

"I'm watching him for a friend," she tells the customers, and everyone buys this story. Even Brendan Fahey finds it plausible, when he detours in for a visit after his bread delivery next door, though at first he laughs and says, "Well now, I thought for a moment you'd gone down to the orphanage and gotten yourself a young one."

She's going to get rid of this baby, this baby who isn't hers—she's going to call the police as soon as she gets these customers out of the way.

Then it's afternoon, and the store is quiet. So is the baby, napping in the crook of her arm, which has begun to ache. Soon it will be time for a feeding, though, and she has neither breast nor bottle to offer. She wonders what his name is, having, when a customer asked, stumbled at first and then, seeing a penny on the counter, blurted out "Abe."

"Hey, Abe," she croons. *Hey, Abe. Hey, babe.* Maybe this is what she's been looking for all her life. She and Abe and Brendan Fahey could escape to Missoula, get a sheepdog, buy a farm. She and Brendan Fahey could change their names—no one would notice amid all the current chaos and the chaos sure to come—and live like that, happily ever after, if there is to be an ever after.

She'll think about this all afternoon, as the sun hangs high above the Manhattan skyline and then swings behind it.

It would all work, this plot, if Brendan Fahey would agree to be someone other than Brendan Fahey and if Evie Myerson could be someone other than Evie Myerson, and if they could pick up and move to Missoula. In Missoula, in six or seven years, a time would come when she would have to tell Abe he was adopted, and then he would want to know the story of his real parents. What to tell him? *Your father was killed when terrorists crashed planes into the World Trade Center, and then your mother came into the vitamin store in Queens where I worked and gave you to me.* Evie Myerson would want to tell her son the truth. But it wouldn't fly. She would have to change it. She would have to lie, and in the end, she was Evie Myerson, who couldn't, and the truth was a story no one would ever believe.

ACKNOWLEDGMENTS

Special thanks to the editors of these magazines, where stories in *Time for Bed* first appeared: "Coffins for Kids!" in *Kenyon Review*; "Portrait of My Mother's Head on a Plate" in *Mid-American Review*; "Tics" in *AGNI*; "BodSwap™ with Moses" in *Normal School*; "Restraint" in the *Cincinnati Review*; "In the Wasp Kingdom" in *The Normal School*; "The Fleischer/Giaccondo Online Gift Registry" in *Indiana Review*; "Love in Wartime" in *Crab Orchard Review*; "The Shift" in *Southern Review*; "The Yak Pants" in *The Normal School*; "Again" in *Cincinnati Review*; and "Outlandish Plot" in *Sonora Review*.

I am grateful for the support of friends, colleagues, and family. Thank you to Michael Griffith for choosing to publish this book and helping me see it with clearer eyes, to Susan Murray and Neal Novak for their expert editing, and to James Long for making it happen. Thank you to the Junction: Carmen, Julia, and Tricia. Most of all, thank you to my husband, Joel Brouwer, whose heart and generosity sustain me always.

CPSIA information can be obtained
at www.ICGtesting.com
Printed in the USA
LVHW112007160719
624287LV00002B/178/P